False Lead

THE GALLOPING DETECTIVE
BOOK FIVE

False Lead

CLAIRE BIRCH

A YEARLING BOOK

For Philip Cowan Merrill

Chapter One

Lucy hurried into the stable office, dropped her knapsack on the extra desk near the front of the room, and stamped the snow off her boots. Jean, the office manager, looked at her sharply from a desk across the room.

"You're late." Jean's dark eyes, rimmed with black pencil, were as fierce as her voice.

Lucy took a deep breath. "For me to get from New York to Oakdale means a bus and a train and a cab. With all this snow everything on wheels is late."

"Then allow for the snow and take an earlier train."

Lucy glared. How many times had she explained to Jean that she couldn't leave her school in Manhattan until three o'clock? Jean's sharp nose and chin were stretched forward like a bird about to peck. A mass of dyed blond hair was piled on her head, held in place by a network of combs.

"Everyone got here but you and your friend Melissa Townsend," Jean went on. "Isn't she coming today?"

"She's supposed to be here, all right. But maybe the plane couldn't—"

"Lay off, Mom. Class is nowhere near starting." Darlene, Jean's fifteen-year-old daughter, strolled into the office from the door to the indoor ring. She picked up her mother's pocketbook. "Do you have a bobby pin?"

Jean took back the large leather pouch and rummaged in its depths. The longer she looked the more flustered she became. As usual, Jean's aggressive manner fell apart when she dealt with Darlene.

"Aren't you staying overnight with Melissa?" Darlene asked Lucy.

"Yes, if she gets here. She went to Barbados with her family for spring vacation, but they were absolutely sure she'd be back for today's lesson. Maybe the snow kept the plane from landing."

Lucy went to a row of velvet hunt caps lined up on pegs by the front door. "My knapsack was stuffed with what I needed for the weekend," she said, "so I didn't bring my hard hat." She lifted a worn black hat from a peg.

"Not that one. It's a wreck," Jean said irritably. "Take another."

"This is okay." Lucy clapped the hat over her brown hair as Jean dug into her pocketbook again.

"Forget it, Mom," Darlene said. "We've got to go."

The tall skinny girl led the way out of the office and into the nearest aisle of stalls. Lucy wished she had Darlene's extra three inches in the legs—the perfect build for a rider. She liked her boyish haircut, too, and her flat little nose that turned up at the end.

"It's the beginning of April," Darlene said. "You'd think we'd be done with snow by now." They hurried along the aisles that framed the large rectangular indoor ring. "You were good to get here at all on a day like this."

"I have to get here. I've lost too much time already."

"You mean you've been sick or something."

"No. My parents split up and I've had to live in New York with my mother this winter. The stable in the city was okay, but I didn't get to do any real jumping or serious training. Before that I'd been riding at Up and Down Farm and—"

"Mr. Kendrick's place in Connecticut?"

Lucy broke into a wide smile. "Have you been there?"

"Once, last summer. Frank took me with him to look at a horse."

"Well, I've ridden with Mr. Kendrick since I was ten. He's a terrific teacher and a really good friend. I'm hoping to move back home this summer and work with him again."

Darlene was silent. Her face, as smooth as china, showed no sign of what she was thinking.

Lucy shifted her eyes to the stalls they were passing and wondered if she'd said too much. "Oak Ridge is a good stable and I like it here a lot," she added lamely. "It's just that coming up from New York is a drag after a day at school."

Darlene still said nothing. A dark red patch had appeared on one cheek, a birthmark Lucy had never noticed before.

As they reached the first back aisle, Lucy saw Buccaneer standing in the crossties. She'd been riding the big chestnut horse seven weeks since starting at Oak Ridge. Jody, the groom, was smoothing a saddle pad over his back. She was a cheerful girl with a broad face and strawberry-blond hair. Lucy was about to jog toward her when she realized that Darlene was talking. "Where did your father end up?"

"My father?" Lucy turned to Darlene. "Oh, he's making a TV series in California. I was just out there two weeks ago visiting him for spring vacation."

"My parents are divorced," Darlene said. "My father's only a few minutes away, but I'm not allowed to see him." Her mouth turned into a tight thin line and she strode off toward Encore's stall at the end of the aisle.

Lucy watched her for a moment, then hurried to Jody.

"Hi, Jody. Thanks for getting him started. I can take it from here."

"Okay. Have fun. He's frisky today."

Lucy reached under Buccaneer's belly for the leather girth and buckled the wide strap to the saddle. She gave the horse a pat. "Good afternoon, mister."

The big horse was broad for Lucy's build, but she enjoyed his lively gaits and his willingness to jump. Since she couldn't afford a horse of her own, she was glad the barn had a few extra horses on which she could learn. The school horses weren't enough of a challenge and the private horses were almost never available. But Frank, the stable manager and trainer, sometimes bought horses like Buccaneer, developed them into stronger performers, and then sold them at a profit.

Darlene, too, had the problem of "looking for a ride." Lucy watched her lead Encore, another of Frank's special horses, into the wide space between the back aisles.

"You'd better move it," Darlene called back to Lucy, and swung onto her horse.

"Yeah."

As Lucy gathered the reins in her hand and began the familiar routine of getting into the saddle, everything else went out of her head. This was the center of her life. Riding. It made her feel capable and secure. She'd had a great time with her father on his TV shoot. It had been a real kick to double in the riding scenes for one of the stars of his show. But now it was time to get down to hard work. She wasn't going to let on to Darlene—or to anyone else at Oak Ridge, for that matter—but her big dream was to ride in the Maclay Finals at the National Horse Show. The competition was intense and the age limit eighteen. With her sixteenth birthday just weeks away, she had to make every ride count.

Lucy urged Buccaneer into the line of horses that made a moving border around the huge open space. As she scanned the ring for Melissa, a short chubby woman with aviator glasses and frizzy hair trotted up beside her.

"Hello, Lucy. I wasn't sure you'd make it today. Take a look at Pipsqueak's new bridle. Isn't it jazzy?"

Lucy caught a flash of purple and green as Eleanor moved past. Little by little, Eleanor was creating a custom look for her horse. The vivid green-and-purple horse blanket had come first. Then the purple-edged saddle pad, and now the crown piece on the bridle. Ellie went to extremes sometimes, but she was one of the friendliest people at the barn.

Lucy turned to look for Eleanor's boyfriend, Norman. Sure enough, he was sitting in a front row of the bleachers. He wasn't a rider, though he kept talking about starting lessons. Whenever Eleanor was at Oak Ridge, Norman was nearby—a stocky blond guy with a raspy voice.

Most of the advanced class was already warming up and Lucy joined them at a brisk trot. She'd been working on getting Buccaneer to move with more "impulsion" or drive. To get the power, he'd have to use his back legs more. She checked quickly in one of the large mirrors at the end of the arena.

"All right, everybody, let's have a sitting trot." Frank walked out onto the dirt floor of the ring. Just then Melissa, perfectly turned out in breeches, boots, and a stunning bulky sweater, rushed toward him. Even from a distance Lucy could see that she was very upset, too upset for something like being late. Her red curls were bouncing as she talked and her delicate hands were moving fast.

Melissa turned to scan the ring and Lucy was sure her friend was looking for her, but Frank put an arm on Melissa's shoulder and said a few words. What could be the matter?

Frank walked to the center of the ring and raised his voice. "Hello there, Lucy. I haven't seen you yet today." Then: "Danny, I thought we were going to try a Pelham bit on Topper. Go back and let Jody help you put it on."

In his early thirties, Frank was six feet tall and extremely thin, with arms and legs that looked as though they'd been stretched on a clothesline by mistake. He reached into a pocket and took out one of the hard candies he was always popping into his mouth.

"Good, Vicky. You've got that back of yours straight at last. That's fine. Feel it. Remember it. Let's walk and canter, now, please."

Lucy put Buck into a relaxed, working canter but her mind was still on Melissa. When Melissa appeared on her beautiful chestnut horse, King Cole, Lucy cut across the ring.

"Are you okay?" she asked quickly.

"Me? Yes. It's the house. When we got home—"

"Don't bunch up, now," Frank called out. "Melissa, move on out away from Lucy."

Lucy tried to speak to Melissa again when the flat work was over and everyone stood at the end of the ring waiting for a turn at the fences. Conversation was out of order, since watching each person's round was an important way to learn. But as Lucy moved closer to Melissa, Danny was already talking.

"Did they take the computer?"

"We don't have one," Melissa said.

"Well, they took mine, and my camera too."

Lucy moved still closer. "Melissa! You mean someone broke into your house?"

Melissa nodded. "What a rotten welcome home!"

"Our house was robbed last summer when we went to my grandmother's at the beach," Danny said.

"There are loads of robberies in Westchester," Melissa said. "But we have a terrific security system at our house. Those guys had to be good."

"All right, Lucy, you're next," Frank ordered. "Now try to keep that strong impulsion you created in the warm-up. I'm not talking about speed, remember. It's more a sense of moving with power. And try to maintain the same rhythm from the time you make your circle until you pull up."

That was the last chance to talk until the horses were put away, and Lucy joined Melissa at the office door. Together they watched the driveway for Mrs. Townsend's car.

"They really cleaned us out," Melissa said. "But the worst thing is the idea of strangers going through all our things. It's creepy." Her blue eyes were serious. "Dad bought me a copy of *The King and I* and I wanted to watch it with you tonight on the VCR, but of course the VCR's gone—"

"The hard hat, Lucy," Jean interrupted.

"Oh, sure. Sorry, Jean."

Lucy took off the hat. A soiled piece of masking tape inside the brim read "Cynthia Bernstein, 14 Riverbank Road." A moon-shaped patch where the velvet was missing suggested why Cynthia had abandoned the hat to the stable.

Lucy popped the hat back onto the empty peg and resisted an impulse to spin it defiantly.

"There's Mom now," Melissa said.

Lucy turned to close the office door behind them. The last thing she saw was Jean fussing over the hard hats on the pegs, lining up the visors just so.

● ● ●

It was eleven o'clock that night before the Townsend household began to settle down and Lucy followed Melissa upstairs to her room.

"Before we go to sleep I have to write in my journal," Melissa said. "We don't get robbed every day!" She opened the top drawer of her bureau. For a moment she stood there staring. Then she pounded the wooden bureau. "Darn it! Darn! Darn!"

"Oh, no! Is something else missing?"

Melissa began to cry. "The locket my grandma gave me when I was born. The bracelet Dad gave me when I turned sixteen. A lot of stuff like that. But that's not—

Look, I'll be right back. I've got to tell Mom and Dad."
She ran out of the room.

Lucy ached for Melissa. She'd been friendly from
Lucy's first day at Oak Ridge and had made it easy to
become accepted in the tight little group of advanced
riders. Lucy thought back to the mysteries she'd helped
to solve already—at Up and Down Farm, at Parkside
Stable in New York, and on the set of her father's show in
California. If only she could help somehow. But a robbery like this was police business all the way.

"I'm really sorry about your jewelry," Lucy said when
Melissa came back to the room and got into bed. "You
can't help feeling sentimental about things you've had
since you were a baby."

"I never thought they'd go through *my* drawers too."
Melissa's eyes were still red from crying. "They'd got the
TVs and the VCR and Mom's furs and the silver—who'd
think they'd want my few odds and ends? That's why I
didn't even look until we came up to bed."

"It won't be the same, I know, but your father said at
dinner that his insurance covered everything. I'm sure
he'll replace the locket and your bracelet and—"

"It's none of that, Lucy. It's the box that the jewelry
was *in*. That was the *special* present." Melissa stared off
into space.

"Who gave you the box? Or is that personal?"

"No. Not really. Did you ever see a movie called
Showdown? It was made here in Westchester and Beth
Stanton, the star, went to school with my mother. They
needed a kid to play Beth's daughter and it was all sort of
a joke because I looked so much like her. Beth gave me
the jewel box when we finished the picture. Even hidden
away in my drawer, it always reminded me that I'd done

something special. And that I would do something special again, I suppose. Anyway, it's gone . . . but I'm going to be in the theater whether I've lost the box or not."

Melissa jumped up and took a cassette from the shelf near her bed. "It's *Red, Hot and Blue,* an old Ethel Merman show by Cole Porter."

"What are you going to play it on?"

"Oh, Lucy. Darn it." As Melissa put the cassette back on the shelf, Lucy thought of her friend Jennifer who'd moved to California. She was going to be an actress too. Between Jen and Melissa, she might just end up with front-row seats on Broadway!

"By the way," Melissa was saying, "did you look at the schedule board for tomorrow?"

"No. Frank's talking to me about teaching beginners in exchange for private lessons the way I did at Up and Down Farm, but nothing's happened yet. I don't really have a reason to look."

"Well, the two o'clock lesson is someone named Peister. There's a guy named Peister who's a senior at school. He's gorgeous, Lucy. All cheekbones, gray eyes, and cool. Believe me, he'd add some excitement to the saddle and bridle scene."

"You sound as though you're bored over there."

"Not exactly bored, but—well, see if you can figure out the secret of my horse's name."

"King Cole? It seems pretty obvious."

"You mean Old King Cole, that 'merry old soul,' right? That's what my parents think too. But for me it's in reverse—Cole is King and I mean Cole Porter." The merriment came back into Melissa's eyes. "He was one of the all-time great songwriters and I love musicals—a lot more than horses!"

"But you've got the most beautiful horse!"

"My mother's idea. I think it was all part of a pretty picture in her head: woman with prosperous lawyer husband and clothes out of *Town and Country,* daughter rides prize Thoroughbred hunter through wooded Westchester trails. Dad puts Mom's fantasies into motion. It's the way it works with them. She thinks up the pictures and he pays for them."

"That's amazing," Lucy said. "You're so—detached. I've never heard anyone talk about their parents like that."

Melissa shrugged. "I figured out when I was pretty little that I was being moved around in those fantasies of Mom's like a Barbie doll. I decided to make up a few dreams of my own and get her to buy into those."

"And did she?"

"Not really. But I dream away. I'm going to step on a stage and—and that second, they'll know I'm a big talent. I'll be set for my own Broadway musical like Barbra Streisand in *Funny Girl.*

"Sure, I'll go to college the way my parents want," Melissa went on. "I'll choose a place with a strong theater department and take King Cole with me. He's my best audience, anyway. I sing to him out on the trails or cooling out. And then as soon as I graduate, I'll find a place of my own in New York and look for—"

"A show? I hope you can find one. Mom says there are hardly any good musicals anymore. They cost too much to produce."

"Don't worry, musicals won't die. I'll write them if I have to. Besides, they'll keep on doing the old ones like

The King and I. Well"—Melissa yawned—"we should really go to sleep." She slid under the covers and cradled her pillow. "How did I get off on all that when we were talking about Ken? I told you before, he's gorgeous. And he's really relaxed, as though he's got nothing to prove. I think he acts older than eighteen. Can I put the light out?"

"Sure." Lucy snuggled under the covers and thought about Steve, the young painter who'd been a teacher at Parkside Stable, where she'd ridden all winter. He'd been too old for her, but she still thought about him a lot. Steve, Ken, or whoever, she couldn't let herself be distracted by boyfriends at all. Getting to the Maclay wasn't going to leave any time or energy to spare. Still, how could she put boys on hold for two whole years?!

What had Melissa said about Ken? Gorgeous . . . relaxed . . .

Lucy fell asleep.

Chapter Two

Saturday morning Lucy and Jody sat side by side in the bleachers of the indoor ring munching on doughnuts from the Village Deli. The stable's top junior riders who rode Maclay classes were warming up before a jumping lesson with Frank.

"Do you know anything about a two o'clock lesson for someone named Peister?" Lucy said.

"Only that Frank said to get Tom Tom ready."

"Tom Tom? The little palomino?"

"Uh-huh. Why?"

"Melissa told me about some friend of hers from school named Peister."

And that's the end of that, Lucy thought. Frank wouldn't put any eighteen-year-old guy on that little horse.

"Where is Melissa, anyway?" Jody said.

"Rehearsing *Carousel* at school." Lucy kept one eye on the ring. "It's great to be around the stable on Saturday for a change. There's time to relax and talk."

"Not for me! I had to bring my little brother and

sister. My mom needs a hand when the kids are out of school.

"Hey!" Jody jumped up. "Those kids promised they wouldn't move from that bench." Striding from one wooden plank to the other, she reached the bottom bench where a boy and a girl, about seven and nine, were trying to climb into the ring. Seconds later she'd brought them back. "Now, you sit beside me like stones or else."

Jody turned to Lucy. "It's hard for them to hang around here all day and stay out of trouble, but what can I do? Every so often Frank insists I work a Saturday. I bribe them with a ride on Tom Tom before we go home."

The little girl was almost a miniature of Jody. Like her big sister she wore her tawny blond hair in bangs, with side pieces pulled off her face into a long switch at the back. But Jody's face was always slightly flushed and her full cheeks were pushed up by her smile. Her gray eyes were rimmed with blue as though the iris had been outlined in pencil.

"What's your sister's name?" Lucy asked Jody.

"Mary. And my brother's Shaun. There are two older ones—"

"And Patrick. You forgot him," Shaun piped up.

"And Patrick," Jody said under her breath. "Quiet, now, kids."

"Tell her about Patrick," Shaun insisted.

For once Jody's face was stern. "I said to keep still, Shaun, and I meant it."

The class was beginning to play follow-the-leader over poles on the ground and low crossrails spaced at different intervals.

"Those kids can't be such good riders," Shaun said. "I could hop over those sticks."

Lucy remembered thinking the same thing when she was a kid. But the truth was that everything you needed to learn about jumping could be practiced over poles and low fences—approaching the jump, releasing the reins for the takeoff, making contact with the horse's mouth again, and moving on to the next jump. Only the actual moments in the air were different when the jump was higher.

"Frank looks like that rock star, Wally Rover," Shaun piped up.

"You think so?" Lucy said. "Maybe the brown eyes and wispy hair. Do you like Rover a lot? I could lend you some tapes."

"Thanks, Lucy, but we haven't anything to play them on."

"Tapes or records either," Mary said.

"Look, here comes Frank. Will you kids be quiet?"

Frank jogged up the bleacher steps. "Lucy, how about teaching a lesson today—an eight-year-old beginner on Tom Tom. Mr. Kendrick said you were 'the best' with little ones, and remember our deal—I'll give you one private lesson for every two you teach."

"That's terrific, Frank. Thanks!"

"Use a longe line and ask Jody anything you want to know. Anyway, Tom Tom's such a veteran, he can practically teach the lesson himself. He's voice-trained, by the way. Don't say canter unless you mean it."

Lucy was truly excited. So the two o'clock Peister wasn't Ken. But Frank was giving her a break! Her family couldn't afford to go all out on the riding the way some of the kids did around here. She'd worked for extra lessons at Up and Down Farm, even before the extra expense of trains and taxicabs.

"You should see Joy Fellows do that," Jody said, pointing to the horses in the ring. "Her legs are so strong, she could ride with a piece of thread in her horse's mouth."

"Which one is Joy?"

"Oh, she's not here. Her mother called this morning. They got back from Vail last night and the house had been robbed. Everyone was up most of the night and no one wanted to cope with driving her over."

"That's strange," Lucy said. "Melissa's house was robbed this week too. And Danny said something about a robbery at his house last summer. It sounds like a lot of people from the stable have been robbed."

"Quite a few, I guess, but there are robberies around Westchester all the time. The stable hasn't anything to do with it."

"You don't think it's weird that all the families have been away on vacation somewhere?"

"People don't usually rob a house when someone's home! What are you, some kind of a detective or something? Watch this kid on the bay horse. He's good."

Lucy forced herself to concentrate on the lesson. Okay, so she enjoyed playing detective, but this rash of robberies was no business of hers. She had her riding to think about. It was the beginning of April, and by the end of June she was going to be working with those Maclay kids down there!

• • •

At ten minutes to two Lucy led Tom Tom to the wide entryway and mounting area between the ring and the huge outside door. As usual, the door was open and Lucy zipped her down vest against the cold air.

A blue BMW came up the Oak Ridge driveway. Lucy could see a tiny girl in the front seat next to a youngish guy. Her "lesson" had arrived.

"Well, Tom Tom," Lucy said, "I wonder what this kid will be like—one who quits in a few weeks or one who falls in love with riding. I guess you've known them all."

Lucy watched eagerly as the car pulled over to the far side of the parking area. A wiry little girl with a blond ponytail jumped out of the passenger door. A tall young man unfolded himself out of the driver's seat. They walked hand in hand to the office. A few minutes later the child ran toward Lucy, wearing a hard hat from Jean's collection. Now Lucy was sure that the person with the little girl was named Ken. "All cheekbones, gray eyes, and cool," Melissa had said. This was Ken Peister, all right.

"Hello," he said. "The woman in the office said we'd find Lucy Hill out here. I'm Ken Peister and this is my sister, Stacy."

Lucy smiled. "Hi, Ken. Hello, Stacy."

Stacy rushed to Tom Tom's head and reached up to pat his nose.

"Easy, Stacy," Lucy said. "Give Tom Tom a chance to know you're there. Come sit down on the mounting block over here and let's talk a minute."

Stacy plopped down on the long ledge on the side of the entryway and waved her feet in the air. "I don't have any good boots yet. Mom's going to get me some."

"Those shoes will do for now. See? They've good heels that won't slide through the stirrups."

"Are you staying, Ken?" Stacy asked.

Ken looked at Lucy.

"We'll be working in the indoor ring," she said. "You're welcome to watch from the bleachers."

"Stay, Ken. Please!"

"Okay, Stace. But pay attention to Lucy, now. You've only got a half hour."

Stacy stood up on the mounting block. "How do I climb on?" She grinned. "I could hold on to his tail and jump on backwards."

"He doesn't steer very well that way. What you're going to do is take the reins in your left hand and then hold on to the front of the saddle, which is called the pommel. That way the reins won't pull on the horse's mouth. Then you put your left foot in the stirrup. . . ."

Lucy demonstrated the mounting procedure carefully and helped Stacy go through it herself. Then she adjusted the stirrups and showed her how to hold the reins. The little girl picked up everything quickly. She was the most energetic, confident eight-year-old Lucy had ever seen.

"Now I'll walk beside you," Lucy said, "and we'll go on into the ring."

Stacy began to kick at Tom Tom's sides.

"Don't do that, Stacy. You're stepping on the gas without knowing how to put on the brakes. Besides, you never kick a horse. You tell him to get going by squeezing his sides with your legs. For now, just concentrate on how it feels to sit there."

"It feels great." Stacy beamed all the way to the far end of the ring.

Ken turned off when they reached the steps to the stands and walked beside them to the end of the first row. He sat down, stretched his long legs out in front of him, and seemed to be watching the other riders in the ring. But his eyes came back to Lucy just as she was looking at him. A slow smile crossed her face. She waved to Ken and turned her back to the stands.

"Stacy, we're going to learn to stop and go. Then we're going to turn right and left. Which hand is your right?"

"This one, silly."

"You'd be surprised. I've taught ten-year-olds who got mixed up with right and left. You're only eight."

"I'm eight. My brother's eighteen. Isn't that funny? He's not exactly my brother. He's half my brother. But his mother lives in Europe and Ken stayed with my father. My father plays the violin and he teaches me to play it too."

Lucy was sure she could learn a lot more about Ken if she let Stacy go on. She was definitely aware of his steady attention just yards away. But they'd better get down to work.

"Stacy," Lucy said, "being with a horse is like spending time with a friend. You want to know him better. You have to pay attention to him. Let's start to do that."

A half hour later, as Stacy went off dancing alongside Ken, her high-pitched voice came back toward the entrance door. "I like Lucy. She's the best teacher there is. Why don't you get Lucy for a girlfriend?"

Lucy blushed. She couldn't hear Ken's answer.

"Frank wants you in the ring." Jean's biting tone broke into Lucy's thoughts. "Leave Tom Tom to Jody and come with me right away."

"Uh—sure, Jean." Lucy hesitated. "Do you know what's up?"

"The ring is only twelve steps away. You'll find out soon enough."

"Thanks a lot."

Someday I'm going to boil that witch in oil, Lucy thought as she walked into the ring. She was surprised to see Frank with Buccaneer. An attractive couple stood beside them and a boy of about fourteen who was evidently their son. He was looking Buck over from ears to tail.

"There you are, Lucy. Lucy Hill—the Patellos: Joan, George, and son Peter." He looked steadily at Lucy. "I'd like you to put Buccaneer through his paces for us."

Lucy smiled feebly and walked over to the big chestnut as Frank brought the reins back over his head. She accepted a leg up and waited for instructions. After all, the trainer at any good stable was the law. She had no choice but to obey. But it wasn't easy to show off your best ride for someone else to buy.

For the next ten minutes Lucy responded to Frank's orders like one of those remote-control toy planes her brother used to own. She forced herself to make the horse look good but she was barely with it. The spring shows had already begun. If the Patellos bought Buccaneer for their son, she'd be even later getting started. Maybe she wouldn't be able "to show" at all. You had to have a horse.

When Frank called her back to the center of the ring, Lucy forced herself to look straight at his eyes as he spoke to her. Frank took Buccaneer's bridle. "Okay, Lucy. Thanks a lot." She dismounted quickly. "How'd you make out with Stacy?" Frank asked.

"She's a natural, Frank. If they really want her to ride, she should have two or three lessons a week."

"Her mother's calling me at five o'clock and we'll talk it over. Thanks again, Lucy."

"Sure, Frank."

Lucy pushed her shoulders back and walked across the ring to the office door. Don't you dare turn around until you get all the way there, she told herself. When she finally turned around, Peter Patello was starting out to the wall with Buck. Unfortunately, he looked great on the horse.

Chapter Three

"**I**'ve made your favorite—stuffed pork chops," Mrs. Hill said as she brought the meat platter to the table on Monday night. "Bring the string beans. They're in the white casserole."

The apartment they'd sublet for the winter was small, but from her seat at the table Lucy faced a large picture window with a glittering view of New York.

"I'm glad to catch up with you," Mrs. Hill said, sitting down at the head of the table. "I'm sorry I couldn't talk when you came in from the country last night. The magazine piece was due today and the outline for the genetic engineering film has to be in tomorrow. As it was, I didn't get to bed until two."

"You've certainly got a lot of things going, Mom." Did that mean, Lucy wondered, that they could afford to go back to Connecticut? Or did it make staying in New York all the more certain? Her mother looked very pretty in a white silk shirt that set off her brown eyes and short brown hair. She must be planning to stay home this evening. She almost never went out on a date in pants.

"Never mind all that. How was your weekend?" Mrs. Hill said.

"Well, I told you about the robbery when I phoned. I felt sorry for Melissa; she lost some things she really cared about. But otherwise, everything was great. I even taught a beginner lesson. Mom, you know all about classical music. Have you heard of a violinist named Peister?"

"Fritz Peister? Lucy, do you really need to ask that? Don't you know who he is?"

Lucy stared at her plate. No one could know everything. Maybe if her mother wasn't always going on about classical music, she wouldn't have reacted against it all her life.

"I suppose Eric would know who he is right away," Lucy said. Her brother always seemed to know everything she didn't. He was a sophomore at college and going into newspaper or TV journalism.

"I'm sorry, Lucy, but Eric probably *would* know. This is what I mean when I say you bury yourself with horses to the exclusion of everything else."

"Well, come on, then, and enlighten me. I suppose Mr. Peister's one of the greatest violinists in the world."

"That's exactly right."

Lucy was stunned. "I gave his little girl a riding lesson Saturday."

"Really? Did you meet Mr. Peister? I didn't know he had such a young child."

"No, Stacy's half brother, Ken, brought her to the stable. I had a great time with both of them. Stacy's adorable. She's got great coordination and she's afraid of nothing. I told Frank she should take at least two lessons a week, even three, if they're really serious. But of course, it would be expensive."

Mrs. Hill's fork stopped in midair. "I wouldn't worry about the cost of Stacy's lessons. Fritz Peister has been a major violinist for at least thirty years. He must be paid thirty or forty thousand dollars each time he plays. I've read that his famous Stradivarius violin is worth more than one million dollars!"

"I had no idea that a classical musician . . . I mean, I knew rock stars made piles of money, but I thought . . ." Lucy's words petered out and she concentrated on her food.

"There's something we have to talk about, Lucy."

Lucy looked at her mother. Her tone was definitely heavy. "Is something wrong?"

"In a way, yes."

"Not Eric! Not Dad!"

"No, honey, I didn't mean to scare you. But it does mean a serious conversation." Mrs. Hill reached for an envelope on the sideboard. "Your school wrote me a letter. You can read it for yourself after dinner, but the gist of it is simple. Several of your teachers have commented that you seem to be overtired. There's a quote here from Miss Porter that 'Lucy is not as quick and imaginative as we've come to expect.' Very simply, they think you're doing too much."

Lucy tried not to shout. "Riding is more important to me than any school. I may not be there next year anyway."

"Lucy, you have to admit that commuting to the stable three times a week is a terrible burden. I shouldn't have agreed. I know your father's all for it—he thinks you can handle anything. But he's on the other side of the country and—" Mrs. Hill shook her head. "I'm sorry. That was unfair. Let's keep this between us."

"Mom!" Lucy could feel her face getting red. "I can tell you one thing. If I'm not allowed to ride, my marks will really be rotten. I'll be so unhappy, everything will just fall apart." The way I'm falling apart right now, Lucy thought. "I've tried so hard. I really have."

"Lucy. Lucy, dear. Somehow we have to make this difficult year work out for *both* of us."

Lucy kept her head down but sneaked a quick glance at her mother. This winter was definitely different. The two of *them* were paired for a change, instead of Mom with Eric, Dad with Lucy.

"Mom, I'm learning to concentrate better. I'm just getting used to studying on the train and in the stable office. My work will improve. You'll see."

"Not if you're totally exhausted."

"But—"

"I've one suggestion," her mother went on. "You do talk on the phone a good deal—"

"I've stuck to the hours we agreed on."

"Yes, you have. But if you cut down your conversations with Allison and Debby, you could add a half hour's sleep each night. Even that might help."

Lucy looked up. "You mean if I was really careful about the phone, you'd let me juggle school and the riding a while longer?"

"Well . . ."

"Mom, you won't be sorry. You'll be proving that you're really my friend."

"I hope so. You're getting closer to college, and your marks are more important now. Exams are only a month away. I'll tell you what we're going to do. I'll agree to the three trips a week to Oakdale. But no horse shows until June. You can catch up with your work on the weekends."

"I don't believe you! Why did you let me think you were on my side only to turn on me like that! How can you be so mean!"

"I thought I was being fair. Concord School wouldn't approve of this compromise at all. You do your best and we'll talk about it again soon."

Lucy swallowed hard. She had no appetite left. "I don't suppose I could go to work right now?"

"If you like. I thought I'd put on a record of the Brahms violin concerto and let you listen to Mr. Peister while we ate dessert."

"Some other time, Mom. Okay?" She got up from her chair and hurried to her room. It was hard not to call Allison to complain. She stared at the blue ribbons lined up across her mirror and wondered if there would ever be any more. Twenty minutes later, when Lucy had finally settled down to her Spanish composition, her mother knocked on the door.

"Ken Peister's on the phone for you."

"Are you sure?"

"I'm sure."

"It's probably about Stacy," Lucy said, but she grabbed the phone in her room. "Ken? Hello."

"Hello, Lucy. I wanted you to know that Marina worked out three lessons a week for Stacy. Will you be able to teach her? She liked you a lot."

"I hope so. I'm only at Oak Ridge on Tuesday, Wednesday, and Friday. In fact I'm not too sure of that right now."

Mrs. Hill walked by the open door. She'd turned on

the hi-fi in the living room. Lucy thought she'd better cut this conversation short or else!

"Lucy, are you there? I'll try to get over for Stacy's next lesson, okay?"

"Sure. Good-bye, Ken. I've got to go. I'll look for you at the barn."

"All right, then. Good-bye."

Lucy had just hung up the receiver when the phone rang under her hand.

"Hi, Lucy, did Ken call? I gave him your address and phone number."

"Oh, Melissa, hi! He called a minute ago."

"Terrific."

"Not really. We talked about Stacy's schedule."

"Don't be dense. He didn't need to talk to you about that. It had to be an excuse."

"Look, Melissa. I'd love to talk, but they're putting the heat on at school about my riding. My mother's rationed my phone time so I can concentrate on homework."

"Oh, no. Well, listen one more minute because I'd rather you hear this from me—"

"It's about Buck, isn't it?"

"How did you know?"

"I rode him for the Patellos on Saturday. So they're buying him?"

"I wish I could let you ride Cole, but my parents would have a fit."

"I know, Melissa. You're an angel even to suggest it. Look, I'd better go. I'll see you tomorrow."

"Sure, Lucy. Frank will work out something, you'll see."

"Yeah. Thanks."

That's just great, Lucy thought as she hung up the phone. Why did this rotten piece of news have to come just *now*. What's the point of getting my teachers and Mom all steamed up when I won't even have a horse to ride?

From her mother's room Lucy heard the typewriter clacking away. In the living room the music became more intense, the violin reaching up and up for the sweetest tones Lucy had ever heard. Her spirits seemed to lift along with them. Maybe there was still some way to pull all this together. She closed the door to her room. Two more months without shows couldn't matter if she kept on making progress. She'd get on top of the homework. Then she'd see about the horse.

Chapter Four

A week later the weather had changed miraculously. The air was warm under a vivid blue sky. From the station to the stable, pink and yellow blossoms announced spring on all sides. As the cab pulled up to Oak Ridge, Lucy wondered when lessons would be moved to the outdoor rings, although with Buccaneer gone that question might not concern her at all. How long could she sit around hoping people would be sick and need someone to exercise their horses?

Lucy geared herself up to deal with Jean. The tension was even worse now that Lucy spent every spare second sitting in the office to do her homework. When she opened the office door, Melissa was waiting at the extra desk.

"You look so happy!" Lucy said. "Did you get your treasures back?"

"I'm happy for *you*!" Melissa said in a whisper. She directed her normal voice toward Jean. "Come keep me company, Lucy. I need a mirror to get my hard hat on right." She led Lucy to the girls' bathroom.

Jean stood at the bulletin board shifting notices into

orderly columns. Heaped on the chair near her desk was a large haul from a recent cleanup—stray sweaters and riding crops, comic books and paperbacks.

"Jean really gets on my nerves," Lucy said, shutting the bathroom door behind them. "You should hear her go on about my books cluttering the desk. She only puts up with it because Frank says to let me work there."

Melissa fluffed her red curls with a hairbrush. "I guess I'm used to Jean. I even feel sorry for her. She's trying to bring up Darlene like a princess on the bits of cash she makes around here. There's some alimony from her ex-husband, I think, but it can't be much.

"Even though my dad's got plenty of money," Melissa went on, "he's always complaining about what things cost. So I can't help feeling sorry for Jean." She zipped her makeup case. "Anyway, forget about her. I heard Frank talking to Jody. You're going to ride Orion, the best horse in the stable."

"Come on, Melissa, you must have heard it wrong."

"Nope. I don't know the reason, but I know it's true. I'll bet you a soda at the Deli that Jean says something as soon as we step back into the office."

"Okay, here goes."

Melissa reached for Lucy's arm. "First, did you hear from Ken again?"

"No, as a matter of fact."

"We were talking in school and I can tell you why. He thought you were brushing him off. Not that he said so exactly, but I could figure it out."

At first Lucy was puzzled, but then she remembered. "It could have seemed that way. That was the night my mother was after me about spending so much time on the phone."

Lucy opened the door to the office, reluctant to have Melissa see her disappointment. They hadn't been friends all *that* long. Would she ever be able to straighten things out with Ken? He hadn't brought Stacy to the stable once this week.

"Oh, there you are, Lucy," Jean said immediately. "Please try to keep the front desk tidy today. I've just straightened up the entire office."

Lucy started to call Melissa on their bet, but Jean went on. "You're riding a horse named Orion today. Jody will bring him to the ring for you."

Melissa's blue eyes sparkled with laughter as they walked from the office to the ring. "You owe me a soda! Anyway, you're going to adore this horse. He's a big dark chestnut almost like Buccaneer, but he's put together like a dream."

Lucy wasn't listening. Jody was walking toward Frank with the finest hunter Lucy had ever seen—even classier than Mr. Kendrick's Moonrock. He walked with his ears pricked forward and his eyes alert, as proud as a winner of the Kentucky Derby arriving in the winner's circle for his blanket of roses.

"Hi, Frank," Lucy said tentatively, feeling that the whole scene might vanish if she ruffled it with so much as a breath.

"Hello there, Lucy. What do you think of this guy? Isn't he something?"

"And how! Uh—Jean said—I mean—"

"Right. We're going to work off one of those private lessons you've earned for teaching Stacy. Come on. I'll give you a leg up."

Lucy put her knee in Frank's hands and accepted his boost into the saddle. As she checked the stirrups and gathered up the reins, she wished Mr. Kendrick were nearby with a few words of advice. This was her best chance so far to show Frank just what she could do.

With Melissa and Jody smiling encouragement Lucy took the horse out to the wall of the ring. She made herself relax, letting her weight sink into her heels. What was she worrying about? This wasn't something completely new, like stunt riding in her father's TV show. She had plenty to learn about hunter seat equitation, but she knew a lot too. "Concentrate," a voice in her head said loudly. Mr. Kendrick wasn't so far away after all.

From the first brisk trot Lucy knew she had to make the most of every second on Orion's back. The horse was responsive but not docile. He had extraordinary rhythm and style. In five minutes she had the feel of his mouth and was moving smoothly from one gait to another.

At the center of the ring Frank and an assistant moved a series of jumps into what looked like a complicated course. No fence was particularly difficult in itself, but there were a lot of interesting turns and changes to manage. Was she up to that?

"All right," Frank called. "Bring him down to the end of the ring, Lucy." There was no putting it off! What's more, Frank was balancing a video camera on his shoulder.

"This setup is a bit tricky," he said. "Go out over the first line of jumps, make a diagonal to the brush, turn back, and pick up the 'in and out.' "

As Frank went on, Lucy followed the course with her eyes while Orion stood perfectly still as though listening to orders. Jody had left the ring, but Melissa quickly raised her thumb for luck.

"Start your circle slowly," Frank continued. "Then

let's see a smooth, even pace with lots of forward drive. He's a hunter, not a jumper, remember. It's not good enough just to get over the fence. Style and manners count. All right, let's go."

As Lucy moved from jump to jump, she felt that every cell of her brain and every muscle of her body was working better than ever before. She was aware of Orion's smallest move and even seemed to sense what he was thinking.

Suppressing a grin, Lucy pulled up at the end of the second round. Her heart pounded as Frank approached. "Good girl," Frank said warmly. "That was a very decent trip. Now let's polish things up."

● ● ●

As Lucy led Orion to his stall, she felt renewed confidence in her riding goals. She'd show them at school. Nothing was going to get in the way.

"So, Jody, I'd better shove off for now." Norman's husky voice was a surprise, since he was seldom back here with the horses.

Jody was currying a ratty gray horse Lucy had never seen before. "Hello, Lucy," she said. "Put Orion in the crossties, will you? I'll get to him next."

Lucy stared at the small hunt cap perched too high on Norman's head. "Does this mean you're finally going to start your lessons, Norman?"

"Getting closer. I borrowed the hat from the office to give Ellie a laugh, but I haven't found her." He ambled off.

"Does he have a job, Jody?" Lucy asked.

"I think he's got some job at the post office that ends

in the middle of the afternoon. He's a nice enough guy, but he's full of foolish questions."

"Like what?"

"Like how do I know which horses to get ready? If someone is sick or away from home, who exercises the horses?"

"*You* do, most of the time, don't you?"

"Pretty much."

"Do you know ahead of time when people are going away?"

"Sometimes." Jody's face stiffened. "Why?"

Had she gone too far? Lucy reached for a way out.

"I came with a couple of questions myself—like who owns Orion and why did I get a chance to ride him?"

"Some people named Storch. They take turns with him, but I haven't seen either of them in more than a week. Jean said something about a car accident. That's all I know."

Jody turned her attention back to the gray horse and began to brush him vigorously. "Tom Tom's ready for Stacy," she added, but she had clearly closed out further conversation.

● ● ●

An hour later Lucy sprawled in the chair behind the extra desk, tired but exhilarated. She'd been pleased with Stacy's balance and control the first time off the longe line. But above all she was excited about her own lesson on Orion. When would she see the playback on tape, she wondered.

The Storches' accident made her slightly uncomfortable. Last summer, at Up and Down Farm, she'd been able to ride a beautiful horse, Silver Whistle, because her

owner needed an operation. Was this going to be another time that Lucy Hill benefited from someone else's
bad luck?

As she called for a cab to take her to the station,
Norman was talking to Jean. The lost-and-found collection had been removed from the chair beside her desk
and he sat there flicking the Rolodex at her elbow. The
borrowed hard hat was back on its peg.

"Why don't we ever see you on a horse?" Norman
said, leaning toward Jean coyly. "You'd look real good
on a horse with that figure and those beautiful legs."

I just might throw up, Lucy thought, but she was as
intrigued as if watching a play on a stage.

"Isn't it a lot of work for you to keep track of all the
riders here?" Norman went on.

Give me a break, Lucy thought. She *can't* be falling
for it!

"Well," Jean said, "it's a lot of work at the end of the
month when the board bills go out. But I'm very effi-
cient. By now I even know almost every address by heart.
After all, I've been doing those bills for three whole
years."

"I think it's time I got on a horse, don't you? How do
I sign up for lessons?"

As Jean explained the stable's payment system, Lucy
watched closely. Jean seemed totally unaware that Norman was continuing to finger the cards on the Rolodex.
Was he just playing with them casually? Or was he reading each address?

"Okay, Norm? I'm ready to leave." Eleanor was
standing in the doorway.

"Hello, honey. I was just shooting the breeze with
Jean here. Thought maybe I'd finally start lessons." Nor-

man strolled to the door, threw an arm over Eleanor's shoulder, and led her outside.

"I don't know why he's always hanging around here," Jean said irritably. "Let him stay in the ring with his girlfriend."

Yes, he'd definitely been reading the cards. Lucy was sure of it.

Frank walked into the office. "Lucy, have you got time to look at the videotape?"

"My cab's due in about thirty minutes."

"That'll do." He deposited a pocketful of candy wrappers in a wastebasket.

"Wouldn't pistachio nuts be better for you? Or sunflower seeds?" Lucy closed her notebook.

"She's right," Jean chimed in. "You eat too much sugar."

Frank ignored them both. "Are you coming, Lucy?"

"I have to pack up my books."

"Fine. I'll be in my office."

Lucy packed up her knapsack quickly. "Good night, Jean," she said, heading for the door.

Jean ignored her as usual. Suddenly Lucy was fed up with her rudeness. She reached up for the first hard hat in the row, grabbed the visor, and gave it a spin. The hat skidded off the peg and fell to the floor. Lucy avoided looking at Jean. Very deliberately, she picked up the hat and started to put it back on the peg. But something was weird. This seemed to be the hat she'd borrowed the week before. Lucy remembered the place where the velvet was worn. And the button had been missing too. But the name tape read "Jill Downes, 44 Cooper Rd."

Lucy hung up the hat and hurried to Frank's office. The VCR was already on, and he sat tipped back in an old wooden desk chair, his long legs stretched out on the desk in front of him.

"Sit anywhere," he said, and started the tape rolling by remote control.

This was the first time Lucy had seen one of her riding lessons on tape. It felt strange, like looking at yourself in a photograph and not quite believing it was a picture of *you*. Frank criticized every detail carefully, pointing out the corrections she'd made from round to round and the weaknesses that still needed work.

When they ran the tape a second time, Lucy watched with greater relaxation. Once in a while the camera swept across the bleachers or the wide entrance doors at the front and back of the ring. An image rushed by that jolted Lucy in her seat.

"Can—may I freeze a frame, Frank?" she said casually.

"Sure. What do you want to see?"

"One frame in that last round."

The problem was how to conceal from Frank what she really wanted to see. Lucy knew how to use a VCR perfectly, but she'd have to seem clumsy. She rewound the tape to the section she wanted where the camera had been angled into the back aisle by accident. She advanced the tape frame by frame. There it was. Norman and Jody together. And she'd been right. In a split second, recorded by chance, Jody was handing Norman an envelope. What could that possibly mean? Did they know each other better than it seemed?

"I can't see," Frank complained. "You're standing right in front of the screen."

"I haven't got the right frame." Lucy advanced the tape quickly.

Outside, a horn beeped three times lightly. By now everyone knew her cab's signal.

"Well, you'd better run along," Frank said. "We covered everything on my mind."

"Right," Lucy answered. "And thanks. I've learned so much today, it's given me real hope."

"You've got more to go on than hope. You've got talent."

Lucy hurried out to the cab, but her mind raced even faster. Tuesday, April ninth, had been quite a day. The misunderstanding with Ken wasn't important. She hardly knew him. Besides, he'd probably have to bring Stacy to the stable again sometime. But she'd ridden Orion. Frank had said she was talented. *And* she was definitely on the track of something fishy at the stable. Maybe she'd find out who'd stolen Melissa's jewel box— or even get it back.

Whoa, Lucy Hill! she thought. Pull back on the reins. You're not going to go in that direction. The police will do just fine without you. She really meant to stick to it.

Chapter Five

Friday, as Lucy looked up from her Latin book, the familiar jumble of buildings outside the train window was dimmed by an April mist. Only the froth of green buds at the tops of the trees brightened the view. She scooped some raisins out of the tiny red cardboard box in her pocket and once again tried to concentrate on her work. For a few days now she'd laid out each day's assignments a new way: Spanish on the bus, Latin or English on the train, time out in the cab, math or history at the stable. Then back again: cab, train, bus. The plan wasn't exactly working yet, but she was coming close.

Flipping through her notebook, Lucy was startled by a page filled with tiny pictures of hunt caps. She didn't remember when she'd made the doodles, but *why* was easy. Had she been mistaken about the hat nearest the door? How had the name tape read "Cynthia Bernstein" one time and "Jill Downes" the next? Would there be still another name tape today?

Lucy thought about Norman and Jody. Jody seemed so natural and open. But as the videotape proved, she knew Norman better than she'd let on. With help from

Jody you could keep track of travel plans for the whole stable. You could line up a neat string of empty houses to rob.

Suddenly Lucy realized the train was slowing down. As the conductor shouted, "Oakdale. Next stop, Oakdale," she scrambled to pack up her books. Her riding was the only reason for this stupid commute and she'd almost missed her stop. Would she get another chance at Orion today? Never mind Jody. What had the videotape shown her about improving her performance? *That's* what she should have been thinking about.

By the time she reached the stable, Lucy felt crabby and resentful. The move to New York had really complicated her life. She marched toward the office ready to bite Jean's head off for one cross word.

"Loo-cee." Stacy peered out of the stable entrance, holding Tom Tom's reins. Ken was standing behind her.

"Be right there."

Jean barely looked up when Lucy parked her knapsack, but Lucy didn't care. Suddenly, she felt happy enough to deal with Dracula.

"Have you been here long?" Lucy said when she reached Ken and Stacy.

"We came early," Stacy said. "Jody let me help her get Tom Tom ready. It was fun!"

"Hello, Lucy," Ken said quietly.

"Hello." Lucy smiled at him warmly.

"Stacy's having a great time at her lessons. According to her, she's practically ready for the National Horse Show."

"You know about the National!"

"Sure. I've gone to see the jumping classes with the international teams."

Stacy tugged at Lucy's shirt. "Come on, Lucy."

"Okay, Stacy. Show Ken how you've learned to mount with a leg up. And come down on the pony's back gently, remember? You're a featherweight now but someday—who knows?" Lucy outlined a fat lady with her hands and Stacy broke up.

Once in the saddle, Stacy turned to Ken. "Come watch me post," she coaxed, arranging the reins. "Let's go, Lucy."

Holding Tom Tom's bridle, Lucy kept the golden pony in place as Ken stepped closer.

"I can't stay," he said. "There are several errands I have to do for my stepmother Marina. But I'll try to—"

"Loo-cee. Come on." Stacy squeezed the pony's sides.

"Sure, Stacy. See you, Ken." Lucy let go of Tom Tom and walked off beside Stacy and the horse.

This kid is wired today, Lucy thought as the lesson went on. Stacy more or less followed instructions and she was really beginning to look good at a trot, but every move was edged with tension.

"Relax, Stacy. You're working too hard. Walk your horse, now, and just relax. Keep your back straight, your legs and hands in position, but let your body relax."

"I'm too excited to relax. Daddy's coming home. My mother stayed home this time, but Daddy's been away three weeks."

"Giving concerts?"

"How did *you* know?"

"Your father's a famous violinist, Stacy. It figured."

Stacy nodded. "He plays the violin all over. Places like Cincinnati and Houston and San Francisco. I can show you all those names on my map."

"Good for you. Now show me another peppy trot. Tighten up those legs. We want them good and strong. Then next week you may be able to canter."

"Today, Lucy. Today!"

"Trot first, and we'll see."

Stacy flashed a brilliant smile and looked straight ahead with exaggerated concentration. Lucy's eyes wandered over the rest of the ring and her stomach seemed to turn over. Darlene had just walked through the back entrance on Orion. Nearby, Frank was carrying the video camera. If Darlene was competing for the horse, Lucy thought, she might as well give up. Darlene was a better rider by far. Lucy forced her attention back to Stacy. Okay, she'd let her canter. Stacy was just about ready and it would keep her own mind at this end of the ring.

Tom Tom was so like a rocking horse that Stacy bounced very little. She hung on with her legs and let herself relax, making a really good job of the first try.

When Stacy was walking again, Lucy asked, "How did you get into the canter?"

"By trotting and going faster."

"Yes, but now let me show you a better way." Lucy looked around the ring and, wouldn't you know, the only example she could find was Darlene. "See how Darlene starts her canter from a walk. She picks up on the outside rein and uses her outside leg. That's what *you'll* learn to do on Tom Tom."

Lucy swallowed hard. "Now look at Darlene again. Which front foot leads the way when Orion canters?"

Stacy stared. "I'm not sure."

"The one on the inside. No matter which way you're going in the ring."

"But how can I tell from up here?"

"By watching the horse's shoulder."

"And if it's not right?"

"Stop your horse and start your canter again."

"Wow! Darlene's got a beautiful horse!"

"You're not kidding," Lucy mumbled.

Ken returned by the end of the lesson and Stacy ran to him shouting, "I can canter, Ken. You should see me. It was easy. Maybe Daddy will come and watch me next time."

Stacy took Ken's hand and she pulled him toward the car. "I'll phone," he called out, but Lucy was too drained to care. How dopey she'd been to assume she'd get a wonderful horse like Orion just as easy as that. It didn't help any that she was about to ride Jill Downes's Pippin again either. That "push-button horse" would go through his paces if you fell asleep on his back. But that was all he'd do. What a struggle for any precision or style. Maybe if she had him long enough for some serious training . . . but Jill would be back next week.

Lucy worked extra hard in class, determined to impress Frank that it was foolish to put *anyone* else on Orion. Still, nothing went right and she was glad to put Pippin away with forty-five minutes to study the causes of the Civil War before she had to leave for the train. The history test on Monday would be her first important mark since the letter from school.

As Lucy walked into the office, Danny and Joy were taking orders for a trip to the Village Deli.

Norman reached into his trouser pocket. "Two roast beef sandwiches for me and Eleanor. And two black coffees."

"That's okay. Pay me later," Danny said. "How about you, Lucy?"

"I could use a grilled cheese sandwich."

"Sure. We'll be back in a flash." They raced for the driveway.

"Darlene looks great on that horse," Norman said to Jean as Lucy took her American history book out of her knapsack. "Come take a look. Lucy can answer the phone."

"Sure," Lucy forced herself to say.

Alone in the office, her eyes flew to the hard hats. Now was her chance to check the name tape without flack from Jean. Lucy hurried to the pegs and took down the cap with the missing button and the moon-shaped worn velvet. She turned it over eagerly. But this time there was no name tape in the hat at all!

Lucy was sitting at the desk staring into space when Danny plunked a brown paper bag in front of her. "Okay, here's the grub. Yours is two bucks twenty-five."

Eleanor walked into the office in her new schooling sweats. They made her look fatter than ever.

"We've a roast beef sandwich for you and some coffee," Lucy said, as she dug into her pocket for money.

Eleanor opened the door to the girls' bathroom. "No, thanks. The coffee will be fine but forget the sandwich. I'm a vegetarian."

"You're a—but Norman—" Lucy stopped herself abruptly.

"Norman what?"

"Nothing, Eleanor. I'm sorry. Don't let the coffee get cold."

What went on with these two anyway? Wouldn't Norman know that his girlfriend was a vegetarian? Was it possible they didn't know each other as well as it seemed?

The phone rang and Lucy picked up the receiver. "Oak Ridge Stable," she said in imitation of Jean.

"Is Lucy Hill still there?"

It was Ken!

"This *is* Lucy, believe it or not. I'm alone in the office. Did your dad get home?"

"Uh-huh. But he'll be away again on Monday and Marina's going with him. Anyway, I've got their seats to the opera. Would you like to come? It's *Otello.* Very intense. Have you read the play?"

"No, but I know it's Shakespeare. I've never been to the opera, Ken. I'd like that a lot."

What an understatement! She wasn't sure about the opera, but she was jumping out of her boots over a date with Ken.

"Okay. If I don't see you the rest of the week, I'll pick you up Monday night at your apartment at seven o'clock. The curtain's at eight."

"But you don't know my address!"

"Sure I do. I got it from Melissa with your phone number."

"Was she in school today? She's not at the stable."

"She's rehearsing almost every day. The juniors and seniors are putting on *Carousel* in three weeks."

"That's right—she's Julie, the lead! Okay. See you Monday." Jean had just walked into the office.

"Who was that?" she snapped.

"Ken Peister, for me."

"I hope you're not getting into the habit of tying up the phone."

Biting Jean's head off wouldn't do. She should be torn apart limb by limb. Lucy's attention shifted to the sound of a truck in the driveway.

"Rick's here," she announced.

Everyone at Oak Ridge knew the sound of the King Cola truck in the driveway and the whir and clang as the back panel opened. Rick, the deliveryman, arrived every Friday to bring new cans and take away the empties. Lucy walked over to the door and watched several of the younger kids race up to Rick. He teased and joked with them as he made one trip after another to the small kitchen on the other side of the building.

Jean pulled a checkbook out of one drawer and a manila folder out of another as Lucy went back to the desk and the Civil War. Soon the office door burst open, and like the Pied Piper with the children behind him, Rick marched in.

"Okay, kids. Where do newlyweds go riding? Do I hear an answer? No? A bridle path, that's where." He swaggered up to Jean's desk, ignoring their groans.

A car horn in the driveway beeped three times and Lucy packed up her knapsack. "So long, everybody. That's my cab."

"Good-bye, Lucy. Next week try to catch my whole routine!"

"I'll do that, Rick."

"Good night, Jean," she said pointedly, and walked out into the driveway. The cab had pulled up to one side behind a row of parked cars.

As she hurried over, the driver called out of the window, "Do you know who owns the Dodge right here behind me?"

"Why?" Lucy asked, walking behind the cab to take a look.

"The tires. See?"

She could see, all right! On the near side of the car

both wheels were resting on the rims. All four tires had been slashed again and again. Worst of all, she knew who owned the car.

"Can you wait for me a few minutes?" Lucy asked the cabman. "I'd better tell someone." She hurried off toward the office, dodging Rick's truck as it backed out of the driveway. Who could have done this? Was it some of the kids, fed up with Jean's nagging? Poor Jean would have to find the money for four new tires.

Lucy called into the office. "Jean, I'm afraid you'd better come out and look at your car."

"Don't tell me someone banged my fender!"

Jean dashed past Lucy and across the parking lot. At the sight of the slashed tires, she let out a wail and sagged against the car.

Just then Frank walked out of the stable. Lucy hesitated at the door of the cab. Jean's blond hair was falling out of the combs. The makeup was streaked on her cheekbones. "How mean can you get," she was sobbing. "That louse! That louse!"

Frank put an arm over Jean's shoulder and urged her back toward the office. "We'll get you home, Jean. Don't worry. Your ex been around again?"

"Come on, Miss Hill," the cabdriver said. "I've other people to pick up and the pack of you will miss the train."

Lucy opened the cab door in slow motion, trying to hear Jean's answer to Frank.

"That's right. It must be him." Jean sounded strangely relieved. "It's the kind of thing that creep would do. He told me if I went after more alimony, I'd learn better."

The last Lucy heard as the cab pulled away was something about "a warning."

Chapter Six

"Allison, I have to hang up now," Lucy said. "Ken will be here any minute."

"Just tell me what you've decided to wear."

"The silk print skirt I got in California and the dressy blouse we bought together before Christmas."

"And your blue coat?"

"Uh-huh."

"Sounds great. I hope the opera isn't a bore."

"Don't worry. I'll be with Ken."

"Well, have fun and tell me all about it."

"Sure. There's this Moor whose wife—"

"I'm not talking about the plot and you know it."

"Allison, *good-bye.*"

Lucy hurried back to her room. When she'd started Concord School, Allison had seemed so cold and outspoken that Lucy'd thought they could never be friends. But actually Allison was very vulnerable and the most loyal friend you could have. Monday afternoon was their steady date because otherwise they hardly saw each other out of school. Today, after the Civil War test in last period, neither one of them felt like doing homework.

They'd wandered downtown and loafed in the public atrium of the IBM building under the lofty bamboo trees, trying to decide what Lucy was going to wear.

Lucy put two thin bangles on her wrist and a light touch of color on her lips. When school was out she was going to get one of those makeup demonstrators in a department store to show her how to do her eyes. They'd looked much greener when the TV makeup man in California had finished with them. As she fastened a button, the intercom croaked from downstairs. Lucy and Mrs. Hill collided in the hallway as they both rushed to answer. Lucy turned back and gave her hair a final brush. She listened to her mother's voice.

"Yes. Yes, I'll tell her. She'll be right down."

Lucy stared at her reflection. Was the blouse too boring? Wouldn't the skirt look more sophisticated if it was longer?

"Ken is having trouble finding a place to park his car," Mrs. Hill said from the doorway. "He asked if you would meet him downstairs."

"Darn it. I wanted *you* to meet him." Lucy swung a beige strap over her shoulder. "Thanks for lending me the pocketbook. I guess I couldn't go to the opera with a knapsack."

"I don't know. I see people in jeans and T-shirts these days, but it doesn't make me very happy."

"Bye, Mom. Will you be up when I get home?"

"Probably. If not, wake me up."

Lucy pecked her mother's cheek. "I can? Really?"

"You *may*."

Lucy looked away. Why was it so important to correct her grammar right then?

"Good night, Mom," Lucy said, and hurried out the

door. When she stepped into the lobby Ken was waiting at the elevator, incredibly good looking in a blue blazer, gray flannel pants, and a bright striped tie.

"Hi, Lucy. The car's parked by a hydrant, so we'd better keep moving."

They hurried to the blue BMW, which looked as if it, too, had been shined up for the occasion. Ken held the door as Lucy slid into the bucket seat. When he'd slipped behind the wheel, he turned to Lucy.

"You look—well—fantastic."

Lucy could feel herself blush. "I had time to put myself together." She tried to think of some way to break the tension. If she looked into those gray eyes for another second she'd dissolve before this date even started.

Lucy smoothed her skirt over her knees. "By the way, I've done some homework for tonight. I read the plot in a book of my mother's."

"We're in luck," Ken said as he started the car. "Luciarotti's singing, and wait till you hear his voice. You won't care whether or not you understand a word."

"Have you been going to operas for years?"

"*Years!* Dad and Marina love the opera and it helps that my own mother's an opera singer."

"Oh? But you don't live with her."

"No, I visit her summers."

"How come?" Lucy wanted to ask.

As the car made its way west, Ken went on casually. "My mother lives in England with her second husband, who's a well-known conductor. I was seven when Mother was divorced from my father. She was planning to send me to boarding school in England but Dad wouldn't hear of it. He thinks English boys go away from home much too young, so he kept me with him, and about a year later he married Marina. I spend a couple of months in London with my mother every year."

"Is Marina a musician too?"

"She was a pianist with a small career, but since she married Dad she just teaches some."

Lucy smiled. "I guess you couldn't escape music if you tried."

"I don't want to. I've played the piano since I was five. The piano means a lot to me and I'll never give it up. But I don't want to play in public. I'd like to write about music—be a music critic, maybe."

It seemed only minutes before Ken said, "Look over there!"

Lincoln Center was glamorous in the soft light of the April evening. Three giant blocks of stone and glass framed a large open space with a fountain in the center. Huge Chagall paintings behind the towering windows of the Metropolitan Opera House were glowing magnets at the head of the plaza.

"We'll park underneath the Met and take the escalator up into the building."

By now Lucy was just floating along, spellbound. As they walked upstairs into the main lobby, red carpeting outlined the sweep of curving staircases on each side. They followed the usher along the aisle to their seats and Lucy was thrilled by the enormous theater, ornate with gold and red velvet, aglow with light from tier upon tier of scalloped boxes.

"That gold curtain's a zillion feet high," she said as they settled into their seats. "How did they ever put that heavy draping at the top?"

"Beats me! I took the Lincoln Center tour one time

and they said the stage was as deep as a city block. It has a revolving floor that can hold four sets at a time."

Lucy gazed at the small crystal chandeliers suspended from cables along the sides of the opera house. Each hung quite low, a fascinating cluster of glass spikes and bubbles. Wouldn't they block the view of the people sitting upstairs?

The audience broke into applause and the conductor took his place in front of the orchestra.

Ken put a hand on Lucy's arm and pointed to the nearest chandelier. "Now, see what happens when the houselights come down."

In perfect unison the two rows of sparkling glass shapes began to rise toward the ceiling. At the same time the lights grew dim. The chandeliers moved up and up until they were flush against the ceiling itself. Moments later the curtain opened and the opera began.

For the next few hours Lucy found herself caught up by the dazzling sets and the beauty of the voices far more than she'd expected. Sure there were long patches where her attention wandered and she found herself especially aware of Ken beside her. Or she thought of Allison and Melissa, wishing they could enjoy this too. She even wondered when her mother had become an opera fan and made a mental note to ask.

Ken seemed to listen with his entire body and there were moments when she felt the music was involving her just as deeply. At times it even seemed to bring them closer together.

During the long intermissions they wandered out into the lobby or stayed at their seats, but either way they talked nonstop. Lucy told Ken about her family, her riding ambitions, Allison, and Concord School. Ken was excited about early admission to his first-choice college and said several times that it was only two hours away.

Each time they came back to the opera, Lucy enjoyed it more. During a terrifying climax in Act IV when Desdemona was about to be killed, Lucy sneaked a look at Ken. His eyes were intent on the action, the angle of his cheek emphasized by the glow from the stage. At that moment he turned to look at her too. Embarrassed, Lucy fixed her eyes on the stage as though her head were stuck on a pole, but Ken's hand reached out for hers and she left it there.

As they left the opera house, the circular fountain in the plaza rose and fell in layered bursts. Clutching her program, Lucy turned for a last look at the Chagalls.

"They've been covered whenever I've been here in the daytime."

"Because of the sun," Ken said. "Look, Lucy, what do you say? The car's safe in the garage. Let's go across the street for a cappuccino."

"Sure! I can't stay out too late, but another half hour won't matter." Lucy looked at her watch. It was already eleven-thirty. It certainly *did* matter but she wasn't going to think about it.

"Well, are you a convert?" Ken asked as the waitress brought the little cups of coffee with puffs of white cream floating above the rims. "Wasn't Luciarotti great?"

"I'm no expert on opera singers but he sounded marvelous to me. And the music made the story so powerful. Now I'd like to read the play and see if I can get into that too."

Lucy fell silent, remembering Iago's evil scheming

and the fiendish way he'd led Otello to misunderstand why Cassio had Desdemona's handkerchief. Then she laughed softly. "I guess not one of the Oakdale robberies with all the loot that was taken caused anything like the trouble of that one stolen handkerchief."

"What robberies? I know about Melissa's family, but—"

"There have been a bunch of robberies since last summer at the homes of families that ride at the stable. And I may have stumbled on the explanation."

"Come on, Lucy. Really?"

Lucy nodded. "I'll tell you more when I've sorted it out."

For the next fifteen minutes they made wonderful discoveries. They both liked artichoke hearts. They both wished they had different names. They both wanted to own Dalmatians some day. Each similarity was filled with promise.

Finally Lucy said, "I'll really be in trouble if we stay out any longer. Will you bring Stacy next week?"

"It's hard now because I'm on the tennis team at school and practice has started. Add that to my senior writing project—" He reached across the table for Lucy's hand. "But you'll hear from me."

Lucy forced herself to look straight into Ken's eyes. It was like the beginning of the evening when they'd started out in the car. But now she felt happy and safe and she didn't turn away until Ken signaled for the check. She thought about Steve at Parkside Stable and Mark in California. They'd been older guys who'd liked her a lot and were *just* good friends. But Ken was going to be a special person in her life. She was sure of it.

They stood up at the same time and said in unison, as if a conductor were standing in front of them, "Thanks for a great time." Then they both broke up and laughed most of the way to the car.

Chapter Seven

"**W**ow! That's unreal." Lucy walked over to the huge black motorcycle parked in front of the tack room wing. Since it was Friday afternoon she wasn't surprised to find Rick standing there too.

"You need sunglasses just to handle the chrome," Rick said. He leaned over to study the instrument panel. "Whose is it, do you know?"

"It's the first time I've seen it here."

When Lucy went on into the office, Stacy slid off the extra desk and pointed to a small white flowerpot she'd been hiding behind her. "The little green things are going to be crocuses," she said. "They're for your desk because you have to work so hard."

"Stacy! What a sweet thing to do." Lucy bent down and gave the little girl a hug.

Stacy pulled away. "Ken helped me."

"Were you supposed to tell me that?"

"No. He said not to."

Smiling to herself, Lucy looked over at Jean to see if she was listening. She was busily leafing through folders on her desk and watching the door, probably for Rick.

"Say, Jean," Rick said, strolling in. "Who owns the black bronco out in front?"

"Some friend of Jody's." Jean reached for Rick's invoice. "How many empties did you credit?"

"It's all on there. It's your count that's wrong."

"So next week I'll add another empty. You had an extra last week."

Rick scowled. "Look, Jean, I can count. And I don't like the way you count."

"Well, that's the way it is."

Lucy was puzzled. Would Jean and Rick really quibble over one extra empty soda can? Jean would.

"What are we waiting for?" Stacy pulled at Lucy's shirt. "I can ride longer today. Roger, our driver, had to pick up Mommy and my dad at the airport."

Rick sauntered over to Stacy and dropped to his haunches so that they were eye to eye. "Hello, little mischief. I've got a good one for you today. What kind of a saddle is best on a crowded trail?"

Stacy cocked her head, thinking hard. She pulled at her ear. "You got me."

Rick beamed. "A western saddle. Because it's got a horn. Get it? You know, in front of the saddle. A horn!"

Stacy giggled and Lucy groaned as Rick clowned his way out of the door.

"Let's go, Stace," Lucy said. "Maybe you can work a *little* longer if Frank is running late, but I have a class lesson and I've got to be ready at six-thirty sharp to go home with Melissa."

Stacy reached out a hand for Lucy's. "Come on. I'll help you get ready fast."

As they walked around to the back aisles, Stacy peppered Lucy with questions about each horse they passed.

Tom Tom was still in his stall, and as Lucy looked around for Jody, she heard arguing from the direction of the feed bin between the back aisles. Jody was talking to a tough, greasy-looking guy in jeans and a black leather jacket. A red devil's head was painted on the black motorcycle helmet under his arm.

For a moment Lucy could make out Jody's voice. "I can't believe you'd come around here pestering me at work. Haven't you dragged us into enough trouble—" Suddenly Jody seemed aware that there was someone in earshot. Turning, she spotted Lucy.

"Let me help you with Tom Tom," Jody said. "I didn't get to him yet." She muttered something under her breath, and the biker took off. Jody seemed uncomfortable, but in seconds she was showing Stacy how to pick out the pony's hooves. Her face was flushed, but there was no other sign that anything unusual had happened. Lucy was intrigued. She'd always assumed that the amiable, steady person she'd seen on the surface was the real Jody. Maybe Jody just knew how to put a good front on her problems. Why had she closed up about her eldest brother, Patrick, that Saturday when the younger children were with her? What kind of trouble had that slimy-looking guy dragged her into? Was Norman any part of this?

"Loo-cee. Come on. You said we had to hurry."

Startled, Lucy said, "Right, Stacy."

• • •

It was six-twenty when Lucy put Pippin away. Next week Jill would be back and Lucy had no idea who she'd be riding, but Jill was welcome to this guy.

"Lucy, are you ready to leave?" Melissa asked as she hurried by.

"Yes. Wait up." Lucy closed the stall door and they walked to the office together. This time Ken was sitting on her desk.

"Hi!" Lucy felt her face light up. "How come you're here? Your driver came for Stacy almost an hour ago."

Ken gave her a radiant smile. "I thought I'd surprise you with a lift to the station."

"What a great idea, Ken, really! But we didn't get to talk yesterday so I couldn't tell you that I'm staying at Melissa's. Since tomorrow's Saturday, I can see her dress rehearsal. Then Frank wants to work with me for some special reason in the morning. I twisted Mom's arm, and my grade on the history test helped."

"Come on, I'll drive you both to Melissa's," Ken said. "And why don't you and I go to the dress rehearsal together?"

While Melissa phoned home to head off her mom, Ken and Lucy had a few moments together by the car.

"That sweater's great with your green eyes," Ken said, giving Lucy a hug.

"Thanks."

They stood together, not talking, just happy to be near each other, until Melissa joined them.

"Darlene's working with Frank on Orion again," Melissa said. "She just came into the ring."

"I've pretty well given up on that," Lucy said.

"Well, then, who are you going to ride? Jill will be back next week."

"I thought they were coming home today," Ken said. "The house is on our way. Let's stop by and see."

The Downeses' large Tudor house was an imposing

sight, as it stood back from the road on several acres. But Lucy thought the dark brown strips of wood against the yellow cement looked old fashioned and gloomy compared to several cheerful white colonials nearby. Maybe she was just partial to clapboard houses because of their house in Connecticut.

"The place looks pretty quiet," Ken said, "but you can't tell much from the road. I'll go in and turn around."

He drove between lawns as smooth as Astroturf. "I think my father would kill for a lawn like this," Melissa said. "He's freaked out by crabgrass. Hey, someone must be home. There's some kind of a van near the back door."

"It's a TV repair truck," Lucy said as they drove closer. "I'm surprised they're here so late."

At the back of the van a husky man paused with a TV set resting on one shoulder. In seconds he shifted the set into the van, slammed the door, and moved around to the front seat.

"I'll go ring the bell," Lucy said, stepping out of the car. She realized immediately that something was wrong. Why was the man wearing a sweatshirt with a hood over his head? There was hardly a breeze in the air.

The van took off at a roar. "Lucy, get back in here!" Ken yelled just as Lucy realized they'd been watching a robbery. She scrambled back into the bucket seat and slammed the door behind her. Ken gunned the motor and chased the van down the driveway. No one spoke and Lucy hardly drew a breath until they reached the road.

"Darn it. I don't see them, Ken, do you?"

Melissa craned her neck from a back window. "They didn't have that much of a head start."

"The roads all twist and turn around here. They'd have been around a bend in no time."

Lucy wailed, "Why didn't I look at the license number?"

"It all looked so natural, that's why."

"Let's go back to the house and find out what was really going on. Maybe the Downeses are there after all. If not, maybe we'll find a window that's been jimmied or an open door. Then we can call the police."

"Wouldn't you think they'd have a burglar alarm?" Ken asked.

"Maybe they do. Some systems don't have sirens," Melissa said. "Besides, we had a terrific security setup at our house, but they just cut the phone wires to the police station and got in and out with everything."

Ken turned the car around and drove back up the driveway. "Even when the alarm's connected," he said, "it can be a while before the police come. The robbers know how to work fast."

He parked near the back door and they piled out of the car. Lucy wandered to a section of the house where the planting was thin and began to study the windows.

"Look!" She pointed to a decal on a window. "There *is* a security system. Why aren't the police here?"

Melissa was at the back door. "Can you believe this? We can just walk in."

They were looking for a phone in the kitchen when Lucy heard the crunch of tires against the pebbles in the driveway. She ran to the window as two policemen with guns at their waists stepped out of a police car.

"It's the police!" she whispered hoarsely.

"Oh, no!" Melissa clutched her stomach.

Lucy swallowed hard. "Look, we were about to phone the police. Whatever speech we were going to make to them then, we can make now."

When two policemen walked in with guns drawn, it didn't seem so easy.

"What's going on here? Get your hands up—all of you," the tall, tough-looking cop said.

Lucy's legs began to tremble.

"Easy, Mike. These kids look all right."

"I'm Ken Peister and I live in the neighborhood. We came by to see if the Downses were back and—"

"We were just about to phone," Lucy chimed in. "That's why we came into the house. There was a van outside and—"

"And who are you?"

"We're all friends of Jill Downes. I'm Lucy Hill and this is Melissa Townsend. *Please* let us tell you what happened. Maybe you can still find the van!"

"Okay, let's hear," Mike said. "You can put your hands down."

"When we drove up," Ken said, "there was a dark blue van in the driveway with white lettering. It said something about TV Repair."

"Bill's TV Repair," Lucy added.

"A guy was putting a TV set into the van, so it didn't seem suspicious at all. But suddenly I wondered why he had a hood over his head and why they took off so quickly. We tried to follow them and at least grab the license plate number but . . ." He trailed off lamely.

"We came back to see if we could get into the house to call the cop—the police. You came just a few minutes later." Lucy finally took a deep breath.

"All right," the bald policeman said. "Come sit down around the kitchen table here and let's go over again exactly what you saw. Then you can leave."

It felt good to sit down, even on a hard wooden chair. Lucy returned Ken's crooked half smile. She and Melissa sighed together with relief. But as they repeated their story, Lucy felt tense all over again. The image of the man with the TV set resting on his shoulder was burned on her brain as if with a branding iron. But what good was that? She hadn't seen his face, even when he moved to the front of the van. And the van description meant nothing. The color and logo could easily be changed.

But both men had seen *her* clearly, standing by the car. And they would certainly remember a blue BMW— possibly even the plates. If the robbers were sure she wouldn't know who they were, she and Ken were probably okay. Otherwise, they were surely in danger!

Chapter Eight

Lucy picked up a stray sock next to her bed in Melissa's room and shoved it into her duffel. Last night, after the dress rehearsal, Ken had invited her for breakfast at his house and he was already waiting downstairs.

"I'm awake," Melissa said sleepily. "You don't have to tiptoe around."

"I thought the star should get her beauty sleep."

"Of course! But I've been awake on and off, escaping the craziest dreams. We watched a real robbery yesterday, you know! Well, before I got through, the man in the hooded sweatshirt was riding a carousel horse."

"So, go back to sleep. You were sensational. Tonight should be a piece of cake."

"Wasn't Timothy gorgeous?"

"The one who played Billy Bigelow? I didn't think about it. You certainly looked wonderful together."

"I've got to find a way to see him after tonight. I will! You'll see."

"You were born to the stage, Melissa. You turned into Julie completely."

"That's what the actress used to say who gave me the

silver box. She had it engraved 'To little Melissa—and big success!' ''

"I wonder what was carted away from Jill's house. I feel crummy about letting those guys get away."

"What could you have done?" Melissa snuggled back into her pillow.

"Nothing, I guess." Lucy gave Melissa a hug. "Thanks again for the berth and loads of luck tonight." She closed the bedroom door softly.

In the hall below, Ken was talking to Mrs. Townsend, but Lucy could tell that he was watching *her* and the ordinary action of walking downstairs was suddenly different than ever before. He was good looking all right, with those high cheekbones and marvelous eyes.

"Good morning!" Lucy said quietly at the foot of the stairs.

Ken cut his sentence short and they said quick good-byes. Outside the door they gave each other an exuberant hug. Ken broke away and took her hand. "I can't wait for Dad and Marina to meet you. And we'd better get moving if I'm going to get you to your lesson at noon. They've got sort of a brunch going at the house, so you won't have to worry about lunch."

Lucy climbed into the blue BMW. "Am I ever going to get into this car again without remembering yesterday afternoon at Jill's? I can't believe I was so stupid. I told you last night about the other mysteries I've helped to solve. I haven't been very sharp this time."

"You also told me that you were going to leave all this to the police and concentrate on school and riding." He smiled at her warmly. "Any time that's left belongs to me!"

"You won't have to remind me."

They drove along the bending roads past one beautiful home after another. Fallen blossoms scattered pools of color on the green lawns. The oaks and maples were now in full leaf.

For a time neither one of them spoke. The car became a special haven like her old tree house in Connecticut, where she could enjoy her most private thoughts and feelings.

Suddenly Lucy was overwhelmed. Being this close to Ken could get in the way of everything else in her life. She wasn't ready to make a choice like that. Solving the robberies was much safer.

"All the same," she found herself saying, "there's something going on at Oak Ridge. I didn't tell you about the hard hats."

"What hard hats?"

"The extra ones lined up on pegs near the office door. A few weeks go I borrowed a certain hat that I'm sure I can identify—"

"Lucy, what are you talking about?"

"The day I borrowed the hat, there was a piece of masking tape inside that said 'Cynthia Bernstein.' I figured it was an old hat Cynthia had donated to the cause. About two weeks ago I knocked the same hat off the peg and Jill Downes's name tape was inside."

Ken had turned his face from the road. "You're sure it was the same hat?"

"I'm sure. I've had an idea that someone in the stable could be tipping off someone on the outside about which houses are empty, and for whatever crazy reason, the hard hats might be part of the system. The trouble is that the Bernsteins haven't been robbed. I don't think they've even been away from home this winter."

"Have you looked at the hat again?"

"Not in the last little while. I've got to find a time when Jean isn't around. She gets really uptight when you handle anything in the office. But a few days after I saw Jill Downes's name, there was no name at all."

Ken was thoughtful. "Did the tape look new?"

"No."

"Who do you think might be leaving the messages?"

"Right now I wouldn't be able to choose between Norman and Jody—though Jody just seems too decent to be mixed up in anything criminal. The two of them may be involved in some way together. You remember when Frank videotaped me on Orion? Well, by accident we picked up Jody and Norman in the background for a few seconds. Jody was passing an envelope to Norman as though she didn't want anyone to see. Supposedly, they hardly know each other."

"What's happening about Orion, anyway? Has Frank said anything else?"

"No, but Darlene's been riding him lately and I suspect I'm out of the running. I'm trying not to think about it and to trust Frank to find me a ride. He's made clear that he believes in my talent and he certainly works hard with me. I think he promised my old teacher in Connecticut to make sure I'd move ahead."

All of a sudden Lucy realized how cleverly Ken had changed the subject. He'd just slipped away from the hard hats and on to the horses. Her ideas had sounded so ridiculous, she couldn't blame him. Should she tell him about Eleanor's roast beef sandwich? There was definitely something crazy about that. Norman was hanging around the stable all the time because of Eleanor. And yet he didn't remember that she was a vegetarian!

"We're the third house down this road," Ken said, making the turn.

Lucy forgot about the stable and watched for the house. "I hope your parents won't mind that I'm dressed for the stable . . . that I'm wearing jeans and—"

"I explained. It's okay."

"In a way I'm sorry it isn't my mom who's coming to brunch. She thinks your father's a fantastic violinist. I mean—she adores music and listens to his records all the time."

"Most people consider Dad one of the top violinists in the world," Ken said matter-of-factly.

"What does it feel like to grow up with a father like that?"

"I suppose it depends on the man. But the truth is, you don't really understand that your father's famous or what it means until you're about ten or twelve. He's just your father. He's a certain kind of man and does things a certain kind of way, like anybody else's father."

"Well, then, what's *your* father like?"

"His world is music and he's extremely reserved, some people think even cold. But Stacy and I know where we stand with him. It's just hard for her having him away such a lot. She can't really understand why it's necessary."

"Does she go to your father's concerts?" They were pulling up to a large rambling house of whitewashed bricks with black shutters.

"No. My father's from Austria. He's spent most of his life in a practice room or on the concert stage, so his ideas about children are still somewhat European and formal. He's always said we had to be ten years old to come to a concert. He thinks it's a long time for a child to sit still and . . . well, anyway, that's what he thinks."

Ken pulled the car into a big garage at one end of the house. "Since it's your first time here, we'll go around to the front door."

They started out along the slate walk holding hands, but Lucy took hers away as they got closer to the door. For a second she felt as if she were at the ingate for her first jumping class at a big show. Then her curiosity took over.

Mrs. Peister was waiting in the large front hall. "I heard the car. And you're Lucy! Hello. We're so glad you could come."

Lucy appreciated the warm greeting. Otherwise Mrs. Peister would have been overwhelming. Marina was about five feet ten, with a beautiful full figure and a dramatic face. Her features were large and her skin faintly olive. Dark brown hair, highlighted with red, was twisted at the back of her head in a glamorous coil. Her huge brown eyes looked straight at Lucy.

"Marina Peister, Lucy Hill," Ken said jauntily. "Where's Dad?"

"Playing duets with Stacy. We thought we'd keep her out of the way at least until you'd had some breakfast."

As Marina led the way toward the back of the house Lucy glimpsed rooms with Oriental rugs, porcelain lamps, and dark, polished furniture. The pictures on the walls were mostly oil paintings like those of the Impressionists she saw in museums. One appeared to be a Renoir. Could it be an original?

A glass-enclosed porch was filled with green plants

and flowered fabrics. At one end a glass table was set for breakfast.

"Excuse me. I'll go tell them in the kitchen that you're here," Mrs. Peister said, leaving them alone.

Lucy looked after her. "She's spectacularly beautiful."

"She really is. I guess I forget about it most of the time."

"Loo-cee, Loo-cee." Stacy rushed into the room.

"I guess the plan didn't work," Ken muttered as Lucy gave Stacy a hug. Behind her was a man of medium height with a long face and sharp features. He was at least fifteen years older than Marina.

Ken stood up and Lucy quickly stood up too.

"Hi, Dad. This is Lucy Hill; my father, Fritz Peister."

"Hello, Lucy." Mr. Peister offered his hand. "Please sit down and enjoy your breakfast. I understand you have to get on to the stable this morning, but I hope you'll spend more time with us another day. Come, Stacy," he said firmly, and they left the room.

It was a strange meal. A uniformed maid served the two of them croissants and an assortment of tempting rolls, a platter of smoked salmon, and eggs cooked to order. Everything was done in a formal way, yet the mood in the house was as pleasant and friendly as anyone could wish. Ken's easy manner helped Lucy relax, but it was hard to talk about anything personal in front of the maid. For a freaky moment she felt as though they were twenty years older and husband and wife. She couldn't help thinking about how different Ken's life was from hers.

"Ken, what's the music we're hearing on the speakers?" Lucy asked.

"Wynton Marsalis, who's probably the best trumpeter in the world these days. He's playing the Haydn trumpet concerto."

"I've heard of him, but I thought he played jazz."

"Marsalis has Grammys for classical and jazz records both. I'll lend you some tapes."

They sat at the table long after breakfast was finished. The moment they stood up, Stacy appeared. "Ellen said you were done, so I knew it was okay."

Lucy patted her head. "I can't stay, but I'll see you at the barn next Tuesday, right?"

Mr. and Mrs. Peister both came to say good-bye. In the garage a few minutes later, Ken opened the car door for Lucy and gave her a hug. He pulled her toward him for a quick kiss. And then another that was longer. When Lucy pulled away, he said, "I knew they'd like you."

"Come on, Ken. We were together all of three minutes."

"So? I liked you after two minutes."

Lucy smiled. "You're a quick study!"

Ken gave her arm an affectionate jab and walked around to his side of the car.

It was hard to say good-bye at the stable. For a while they just stood and looked at each other. Lucy started to walk away, then found herself turning back. Ken put his arms around her and said against her ear, "I'll call you tonight. But somehow, *I've* got to leave and *you've* got to go ride. When I let go, we both walk away."

"Okay, okay," Lucy said.

"So, here goes."

Lucy walked off toward the barn without looking back.

When she walked into the indoor ring, Frank was

riding the new gray horse she'd seen Jody grooming. Two weeks had made a big difference. He'd filled out and his coat was in much better shape. She could see quickly that he had a nice way of moving but a strange habit of turning his head as he came into a jump. Why had Frank made a special point of wanting to see her this morning? Who was *she* going to ride? Did she dare hope that Orion would be brought to the ring?

Frank jumped one more fence and trotted over. "Lucy, I want you to ride this horse today. Work with him on the flat so I can see him move. We'll talk about it later."

Lucy clenched her teeth and tried to hide her disappointment.

"What's his name?" she asked, as Frank handed her the horse.

"I don't know yet." He pulled a bag of candy out of his pocket and tore it open. To Lucy's surprise the gray horse shied away from the sound. Lucy looked at Frank.

"He's been blinded in his left eye, so he spooks easily at noises on that side."

"Then how can he jump decently?" Lucy said.

"By previous experience and by turning his head slightly. Right now it's more than slightly, but we'll help him with that."

Lucy tried not to look disappointed, but it was tough enough to lose out on a perfect horse like Orion without ending up with one that was half blind!

"This horse is a real chance to learn," Frank said. "I saw him in a paddock upstate when I was buying jump standards from a guy who was moving to Arizona. He didn't know much about the horse except that his eye was injured in a trail accident and then he'd been sold a few times. He'd hardly been ridden in months, but I watched this gray fella move around the paddock and something made me take him home.

"Come on, Lucy. Climb aboard." Frank cupped his hands. "I've been working him down each day and you'll do fine. Ride him for me a half hour or so, make your hand and leg signals decisive, and we'll talk about it all on Tuesday."

"Sure, Frank." What else could she say?

Thirty minutes later Lucy was definitely encouraged. The horse's trot and canter were great. She'd followed Frank's instructions and worked at making each signal precise. When the horse's blind eye was on the outside, she'd had to use a strong inside leg to keep him from moving toward the center of the ring. It had been a challenge. But the big question was still ahead. How would they make out over fences?

Lucy handed the horse back to the groom and headed for the soda machine in the old stable kitchen. Her thoughts drifted back to Ken, his parents, his home —and how different their life was from hers. What was it like to grow up with all those servants, to live part of each year in London?

Several of the youngest kids were standing at the pay phone near the soda machine. A dark-haired girl held out a small piece of paper. "Look, Lucy."

The word MEMO was printed at the top. The next Monday's date was typed underneath, followed by the names of several stable families.

"Where did you get that?" Lucy asked lightly.

"Eleanor's boyfriend," the biggest boy answered. "He was using the phone and it dropped out of his pocket when he left."

"I'll take care of it." Lucy reached for the paper and put it in her pocket. She bought herself a soda and leaned against the wall drinking it slowly, as the kids gradually took off.

Did she now have proof that Norman was supplying the names to the thieves? She couldn't resist any longer. She had to solve this mystery! Her mother had often said that the busiest person can always handle one thing more. Well, maybe she could live up to that notion if she tried. From the opera Monday night to the brunch this morning, this week had been unreal. She felt stronger and happier than ever before. Why not try to do it all!

Chapter Nine

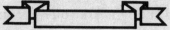

When Lucy arrived Tuesday afternoon, Frank was in the office emptying out candy wrappers from his pocket. Stacy sat on the desk watching.

"Frank, how come you eat so much candy and we can't feed sugar to the horses?"

"Because I brush my teeth three times a day and they don't."

Stacy rolled her eyes at Lucy.

"Lucy, when you finish with Stacy," Frank said, "tack up the gray horse yourself. Make friends with him. Then warm up awhile and when I finish the Intermediates, we'll get together."

"Sure, Frank." Lucy watched him leave the office. She'd tried to sound cheerful. Every other part of her life was zooming. Ken had been calling every evening; in fact her mother had begun to complain again about the phone. She'd finally managed a Latin translation with only one mistake and her Jane Austen paper had earned the best teacher comment she'd had all year. Since riding meant more to her than anything else, she was going to get her act together on that gray horse, and that was it!

"Lucy, you're not answering me."

"I'm sorry, Stace, I was miles away. What did you say?"

"Before you came, some of the kids were talking about a horse show. How old do I have to be to ride in a horse show?"

"You're old enough. Are you *ready* enough, that's the question."

"If I work real hard. Can I, maybe?"

Why not, Lucy thought. There was a schooling show only forty-five minutes from Oak Ridge at the end of the month. These were small unofficial shows, designed to help kids and even grown-ups get early horse show experience. There were extra classes for beginners, like "lead line," in which instructors led their pupils' horses as they walked or jogged beside them.

"Tell you what, Stacy. I'll talk to Frank. If you work hard and we decide the answer's yes, I'll lend you one of my good-luck chokers to wear around your neck."

Stacy's eyes were sparkling as they went for Tom Tom. She cut out the clowning for the entire lesson and followed every instruction right away. When they brought Tom Tom back to his stall, everyone in earshot had to hear that she'd cantered on the right lead every time.

"You mean the outside foot was always moving forward?" Jody asked with a serious face.

"Jody, don't you dare," Lucy protested with exaggerated anger. "Don't mix her up."

"The *inside* foot goes ahead," Stacy said solemnly. "I listen to Lucy. You're putting me on the wrong lead."

"Come on, Stacy," Lucy said, "I'll show you the new horse I'm going to be riding."

"What's wrong with his eye?" Stacy asked at the stall. "It looks all funny. See? Over there."

"He's had an accident and that eye is blind."

Stacy closed one of her large brown eyes and stared at Lucy with the other. "He must *feel* funny too."

Roger collected Stacy, and Lucy settled down to make friends with the gray horse. First she looked him over carefully. She spoke to him in a calm voice and moved from one side of his head to the other. Suddenly she realized that she was closing one eye the way Stacy had done. "He must feel funny too." What did they say— out of the mouths of babes?

You've been so busy worrying about yourself, Lucy scolded, you haven't thought about this poor animal at all. He must feel very insecure now in a busy ring and especially when he's coming up to a fence. "I'm going to be your friend," she crooned as she led the horse to the crossties. He really had a sweet disposition. That was easy to see from how willingly he moved aside or allowed her to lift his feet. Maybe she could win his trust and serve as sort of a second eye. Then when she gave him the signal to jump, he might just take off and not bother with turning his head.

"I'll see to it that you get a second chance, that's what," Lucy said as she brushed the horse's shoulders. Then she started to laugh. "But you're really my second chance too. Without you I'd probably be riding the tack room saddlehorse in the June shows." She brushed the horse's legs one after another. Suddenly she stood up straight and looked him in the eye. "I know what to call you! It's perfect." She rubbed his nose. "I christen you Second Chance."

• • •

"It's depth perception that he's lost," Frank said when they got together in the ring. "You need two eyes for that. We're going to approach this problem two ways. We'll rebuild his confidence about judging distance by a lot of work over low jumps in different combinations. At the same time we'll build his trust in *you*. You'll be surprised how much that will mean.

"You were hoping to ride Orion, I know," Frank went on. "But the Storches looked at your videotape and Darlene's and decided to go with her. I'm sure part of it was that they want to show the horse all summer and you may not even be at this barn. Anyway, don't be discouraged. You're going to learn more from this horse than you ever could from Orion. Wait and see. Would you like to name him for me?"

"I already have. Frank London, meet Second Chance!" They laughed together and got down to work.

Later, when Lucy was bolting the door to Chance's stall, Darlene walked over. "I wanted to tell you I'm sorry I had to win out over *you* for Orion. I think you're a terrific rider."

What a nice surprise, Lucy thought as they walked along together, their boots echoing against the concrete in the aisles.

"I'm going to the Deli with Joy and Danny. Want to come?"

"No, thanks. Another time, though."

Right now Lucy wanted to hang around the office until train time. If Jean was away from her desk, she'd take another look at the hard hat. If not, there were questions she wanted to ask.

"Mom, I need some cash," Darlene said as soon as they reached the office.

Jean dug into her purse but muttered, as Darlene left, "That girl just eats money."

Lucy pulled some books out of her knapsack along with the list the kids had found by the pay phone. A photocopy was safe in her night table at home. After pretending to read awhile, she brought it over to Jean.

"I've been meaning to give you this. It was lying on the floor near the pay phone the other day."

Jean's chin jutted forward. "What's that?" she snapped, grabbing the note. "Oh, is that all? I make a list like that for Frank and the grooms every week. I keep my copies right here in this drawer. I don't know what the rest of them do with their lists, but they certainly shouldn't end up on the floor."

Lucy went back to her desk. "What do you do if things change?" She was trying to sound casual. "What happens if a family plans to be away and then doesn't go?"

"Isn't that a stupid question! You're beginning to sound like Norman. If people change their minds, they show up at the stable and ride their horses. What do you think happens?"

Jean was getting annoyed. Lucy looked for another approach.

"I'm really happy for Darlene, Jean. She's a beautiful rider and she deserves the opportunity with Orion. But I thought if you could give me an idea who was going to be away from time to time, I might get a chance to ride a really good horse and—"

"Isn't that up to Frank?" Jean said sharply. "Besides, isn't he counting on you to ride the new gray horse?"

To Lucy's relief Cynthia Bernstein rushed up to
Jean's desk. "Frank wants you to schedule an extra private lesson," Cynthia said. "He thinks my sense of
rhythm's gone haywire and . . . Hey, I'm sorry. I guess
I interrupted."

"We were finished," Lucy said quickly. "Say, Cynthia,
could we go to the Deli for a sandwich? I'm starved, and
besides, I need to talk to someone about 'showing' with
Oak Ridge. The Woolcott Show will be my first time
and . . ."

Fortunately, Cynthia agreed. As they walked toward
her car, Lucy took a deep breath. She hoped they
wouldn't run into Darlene at the Deli. She'd hate to hurt
her feelings. But she was glad to get away from Jean
before things got too sticky. Besides, she'd been wanting
to speak to Cynthia for weeks, and not about horse
shows.

• • •

"The Deli is really the local clubhouse," Cynthia said
as they walked past the sausages and cold meats, the
rows of salads and pastries, into the maelstrom of sound
at the back. Kids from the stable and the high school
dashed in and out. Lucy and Cynthia slid into a high-
backed booth, and the waitress took their order almost
before their jeans touched the wooden seats.

"I watched you ride today while I was warming up the
new gray horse," Lucy said. "You're really determined. I
could see it."

"Thanks, Lucy. I've been riding since I was nine, but
I'm not very talented. I should be much better by now."
Cynthia's violet-colored eyes were huge and bulged so
far forward that they seemed to reach out toward you

when she spoke. She shifted her heavyset body against the back of the booth. "I just keep on trying. I love to ride even if I'm a klutz."

"I used an old hard hat of yours one day. I guess you donated it to the stable."

"Yeah—a few of them by now, in ascending sizes."

"This one had your name and address in it written on masking tape."

"I never paid any attention. My mother could have done something like that."

The waitress brought Lucy's grilled cheese sandwich and Cynthia's milk shake. Lucy decided to leave the hard hats alone and find a way to get to her most important question. Meanwhile the conversation rambled.

"There's one way I'm great on a horse," Cynthia said, laughing. "I can say 'whoa' in French, Spanish, Italian, and German."

"You really can speak four foreign languages? How'd you manage to learn them all?"

"They just stick to me. I learned the French when I was little from someone who worked in the house, then I taught myself Spanish from translations of kids' books, like *A Bear Called Paddington* and *Winnie-the-Pooh*. The German and Italian I've been taking in high school. The trouble is, I'd trade it all to ride like you."

"Maybe you won't always feel that way. All those languages will probably get you into a great college, and think of the jobs you'll get later!"

"I know. I'd still rather ride like you."

Lucy took another bite of her sandwich. "Cynthia, have you traveled in any of those countries—like France or Italy, I mean?"

"Mexico and France. But my parents are going to

send me to Europe this summer on a riding junket through Spain." Her broad mouth broke into a smile. "They're always pushing the languages, and I'm pushing the riding. We got it together for the month of August."

"I thought your family was going to Mexico about a month ago. Did you go or am I wrong?"

"Mexico? No. After that one trip my father said he'd never go again. It was too bad because all the rest of us loved it—four against one."

Now what? Lucy searched for a new angle.

Cynthia slurped the last drops of milk shake at the bottom of the glass, then looked up from the straw.

"We were supposed to go to Bermuda a while ago, but my father had some business problems and couldn't leave."

"When was that? You must have been terribly disappointed."

"Not particularly. It was during spring vacation, so I was able to ride every day."

"Melissa's family was robbed during spring vacation. Joy's too. You may have been lucky."

"My mother was furious. We were all packed and everything."

"Sometimes robbers get tipped off about families that are going away. You know, that's why they tell you to cancel the newspapers so they don't pile up at the door. But maybe the newsdealer feeds those names to someone. I was just wondering if anyone tried to break in and then realized you were all still at home. Were there signs of that at all?"

"Hello, Lucy. Cynthia. How'rya doin'?" Eleanor had materialized at the end of their booth as though from a trap door in a magic act.

Behind her came Norman. "Hello, kids. Taking time out, I see."

Lucy gulped. They must have been in one of the booths along the same wall. Just how far away had they been? How much had they overheard?

While Cynthia talked on, Lucy watched Norman and Eleanor walk to the cashier at the front of the store.

"No. We've never had any trouble at all," Cynthia said.

For a moment Lucy didn't know what Cynthia was talking about. She was too concerned that Norman and Eleanor had overheard their conversation. If the robbers at Jill's house knew who she was, she was already in danger. If they thought she was onto them . . . Had she just made matters worse?

Back at the stable Lucy waited outside for her cab and tried to relax, enjoying the fresh spring smells in the air and the pleasure of bright light so late in the day. As she paced up and down beside the parked cars, she thought of the time Jean's tires had been slashed. Nothing more had been said about it.

Impatient with waiting, Lucy tried to see how many cars she could match up with their owners. The red Honda Civic looked like Jody's. Right. It had a Bradford College sticker on the windshield. Jody had gone there before taking this year off. On the backseat Lucy noticed two large boxlike shapes covered with a blanket. She walked closer to the window. The corner of an AR hi-fi speaker was showing, the kind Melissa's parents had lost from the living room. Lucy remembered the conversation with Jody and the kids. "We haven't anything to play them on. Tapes or records either."

Well, they did now! What did it mean? Lucy felt as if

she were holding a kite that had just lifted into the wind. These weren't brand-new speakers. Otherwise they'd be in a box. Could this be part of the payoff for tips to the robbers?

The cab came minutes later and Lucy tried to make herself study on the way to the station, but there was too much else in her head. The conversation with Cynthia had really wrecked the hard hat angle. The break-in at Jill's house was probably just a crazy coincidence. Besides, Norman seemed to be supplying names by phone and Jody was putting her messages into envelopes if the videotape was any indication.

As the cab arrived at the station, the train was just pulling in. Lucy raced for the platform, swung aboard, and settled down in the first empty seat. Now she was going to get down to work. She opened her notebook and her heart seemed to stop. A new page had been clipped into the notebook ahead of the others. Bold black letters read:

**STOP MAKING TROUBLE
OR YOU'LL BE SORRY**

Chapter Ten

After so many meals alone with her mother in front of the big picture window, Lucy found it strange to have her brother, Eric, there with them. But what a terrific surprise for her birthday. The seventeenth of May had arrived. She was sixteen at last.

"Well, Luce," Eric said. "No more waiting to be chauffeured back and forth to the stable. You'll be able to drive now."

"I can't wait. But where am I going to learn?"

"How about Connecticut?" Mrs. Hill said with an impish smile.

"Mom! Are you trying to tell me something? Mom!"

Lucy felt like racing from one end of the apartment to the other like a colt in a paddock. She grabbed the seat of her chair with both hands. "So tell me straight out. I can't stand it."

"I don't know yet whether it will be July, August, or September, but yes, we'll be going back home."

Lucy's excitement suddenly fell flat. She'd wanted to go home so badly, and yet she felt uncomfortably hollow. Her father wouldn't be there. Eric wouldn't be there.

What would it be like in that big old house—just the two of them? Luckily, Ken could easily make the drive from Oakdale in about half an hour.

"So tell me what's going on," Eric said, cutting into the large slice of roast beef on his plate. "I was hoping to meet Ken tonight."

"Mom hasn't met him yet either. He's graduating from high school in a few weeks, so he's got lots to finish up. Besides, my birthday didn't seem like the best time."

"I hear he's Fritz Peister's son."

Lucy blushed. "What else did Mom say?"

"Eric, you're not giving her a chance to eat."

"You mean she doesn't talk with her mouth full anymore?"

Lucy made a face. "You mean you're still as obnoxious as ever?"

"Of course. But I'll leave you alone for tonight."

Lucy threw Eric a quick smile. "The trainer at Oak Ridge is really good," she said. "I've got my usual problem of finding something to ride, but right now I'm working with a horse who's been blinded in one eye and it's interesting—he's really beginning to trust me. If Mom lets me ride in the Woolcott show a week from Saturday, I might finally make it out of Limit into Open. I only need two more blue ribbons."

Eric looked at Mrs. Hill.

"It depends on her final exams."

"Come on, Mom. Has she been doing badly in school?"

"This last month has been exceptionally good, but—"

"But it took me time to get used to the commuting, that's all."

"I'm not worried, Lucy," Mrs. Hill said. "To tell the truth, I've told Frank to go ahead with the entries."

Lucy looked at her mother in disbelief. The ring of the telephone broke up her reaction.

"Lucy, it's probably for you. Have you seen her room, Eric? It's filled with flowers from Allison and Ken and . . ."

Lucy raced for her room and grabbed the phone.

"Hello, honey. Sixteen big hugs and one to grow on!"

"Hi, Dad. I thought it would be you."

"How goes it?" he asked.

"The same as when we talked last Sunday. Everything's fine, except that I miss you."

"Nothing's the same. You're sixteen now!"

"I'm not used to it yet. It's only been a few hours."

"I guess not."

"Could I call you later tonight? The trouble is that we're in the middle of dinner. Eric's here and—"

"Of course. Or we'll catch up Sunday night the way we always do."

"You know Mom's talking about going back home."

"She told me. Aren't you pleased?"

"Yes. . . . I don't know. I'm not sure anymore."

"Well, enjoy your birthday, honey, and we'll talk about it later. Did you get my present?"

"No, not yet."

"*No!* What's the matter with that store? They promised it would be at the apartment yesterday at the very latest."

"Well, don't worry, Dad. Do you want to tell me what it is?"

"What have you been after for the past two years?"

"You didn't! Not an Hermes saddle!" Lucy sat down on the bed. "Oh, Dad! How do I thank you!"

"Back to the table, honey. If it hasn't arrived by tomorrow, I'll tear that place apart on Monday."

"Sure, Dad. Look, it doesn't matter that it's not here. I know it's coming, and that's enough."

"So long, then."

"Right." After she hung up the phone, Lucy sat on the bed quietly. The feeling that her family was split in half wasn't quite so painful anymore. But would she ever stop wanting to be in two places at once?

• • •

When Mrs. Hill went back to work, Lucy and Eric stood at the big window looking out at the city.

"It's magical," Lucy said, "but I can't walk out there late at night by myself."

"You want to take a walk?" Eric said. "Let's go!"

They strolled together to the East River and up the river promenade from Seventy-ninth Street. Eric's long face and black hair, even his way of walking, were so like her father's, it made Lucy miss her father even more. Funny about her brother, she thought. They'd fought a lot and they were very different. But they were becoming better friends as they got older and they would always have each other. Brothers and sisters didn't get divorced.

Near Gracie Mansion, the big white house where the mayor of New York lived, they sat down on a bench that faced the water.

"We haven't had a good long talk since last summer," Eric said. "You were deep in the mystery at Up and Down Farm."

"There's no way to catch up with you. You're either at school or working on a newspaper somewhere miles away."

"Well, this summer it's Watertown, Connecticut. That's not far away at all. There's a good small paper there and I'll be filling in for the reporters on vacation."

"Now, *that's* a birthday present!"

"Did you turn in your detective badge after the triumph in California? I heard about it from Dad."

"Not exactly. Believe it or not, I'm in the middle of something now. But I can't make it come together. Besides, I . . ."

Her voice drifted off. The river was dark and mysterious, bouncing back the tantalizing lights from both shores. She stared at the view and let her mind go blank.

"What's up, Luce? Tell me."

"I've a lot of things to balance right now. School, riding, and—well, my first real boyfriend—I mean—I suppose this must be the way you feel when you're falling in love."

She looked at Eric, expecting a teasing remark, but he was smiling at her fondly. After a moment she went on. "It's tougher getting back and forth to the stable than anyone realizes and three days a week really isn't enough riding, so I keep pressing for more—" She stopped. "And then—"

"What? There's something else you're not telling me."

"I don't want to exaggerate, that's why. In fact, the warning may have been a joke. It was almost a week ago now, and there's been no sign of trouble."

"What warning?"

"A surprising number of families have been robbed

at Oak Ridge, the stable where I'm riding now. I'm convinced that someone is giving out tips from the stable about who's going to be away from home. It could be a guy named Norman. Or a girl groom named Jody. Or even Jean, who manages the office. . . ."

Lucy went on to tell Eric about the hard hats, about Norman's inquisitiveness and the piece of paper near the phone—about Jody and Norman on the videotape, the biker by the feed bin, the hi-fi in the car. Again she stopped short and gazed at the Triborough Bridge. Its lights were suspended over the river like a giant necklace worn by the darkness.

"Lucy," Eric said. "Do I have to resort to torture? You're *still* holding out on me."

"Ken, Melissa, and I interrupted a robbery at Jill Downes's house. It was a complete coincidence, and we were pretty dumb about it—that's a long story—but the men who did the job got a good look at Ken's BMW and certainly at me.

"Then last week I was pretty stupid again. I was down at the Village Deli talking to one of the kids about the robberies and trying to get some information I needed, when I found out my prime suspect might have been in the booth behind us. The backs of the booths are very high, which had thrown me off guard, but they're not very solid.

"Well, my schoolbooks are almost always on a certain desk in the office. I have to study every second I get—between lessons, anytime. Everyone knows that by now. Later, when I opened my notebook on the train, there was a warning—big block letters telling me to lay off or I'd be sorry."

Eric cracked his knuckles, which usually meant he was thinking hard.

"It's been calm up there all week," Lucy hurried to say. "No sign of any trouble at all. I've just about decided Cynthia Bernstein, the girl I was questioning at the Deli, might have put the page there as a joke. Mostly, I'm angry at myself. And if I'm going to be in danger, I'd like it to pay off."

"Who's in the office regularly? Isn't there an office manager, like at Kendrick's?"

"I told you, that's Jean. She's a real pain. Much too fussy. She's definitely hard up for money. I know she was trying to get more alimony from her husband. She's got a daughter who rides at the stable, and I suppose Jean gets some of that as a job trade-off, but still . . ." Lucy thought a moment. "The note sounded like her too. I think Norman would have written something tougher than 'Stop making trouble or you'll be sorry.' "

"So you think Jean could be using the hard hats to carry messages? Then who's picking them up? If it's Norman, why doesn't she just give him the info? And if they're in this together, why does he have to be so inquisitive?"

"Maybe it's Jody, then. I told you it was confusing!"

"Who runs the place? You're making Oak Ridge sound like a den of thieves."

"Frank London's the manager and trainer. I've never suspected him for a second. That would be crazy." She shook her head vigorously. "But you're right. He knows who's going away as much as Jean. She gives him notes."

Eric leaned back against the bench and put an arm around Lucy's shoulder. "Forget the hard hats, Luce. They're just in the way. There's some sort of a dumb explanation, and since the last label came off, there hasn't been a new one. The Jill Downes thing was just a coincidence."

"You're probably right."

"In fact, I think you should forget this particular 'case' altogether. You've lost a lot of time from your riding. I can't tell you what to put first, but if we're going back to Connecticut and you can ride with Mr. Kendrick every day, you'll have a fair shot at the National. You've put years into that dream. You've already got a lot on your plate, and now you're in love too."

"That's got nothing to do with it."

Darn it. That's what always happened with Eric. Just when she felt close to him, he'd go and ruin everything.

Lucy stood up. "We'd better get home. I've still got thirty pages to read tonight."

Eric stood up, too, and grabbed her arm. "Hey, Luce, I'm on your side, remember?"

"Yeah . . . I know . . ."

"A whole winter alone together and Mom hasn't cured you of saying 'yeah' yet?"

"She's definitely trying. I go around half the time saying 'Yeah—I mean yes,' like someone with a tic."

"Not to me. I get 'Nope—I mean no.' Think about what I said, okay?"

"Will I get to preach to you someday too?"

"Just watch for your chance!"

They walked away from the river and the magic of the evening was over. But she was sixteen—and there was Ken—*and* her mother was going back to Connecticut. That was magic enough for months to come.

Chapter Eleven

On the train the next day every Spanish verb seemed to echo the conversation with Eric at the river. *Ir,* "to go." Where should she go next with this muddled mystery? *Amar,* "to love." Of course she wasn't *really* in love with Ken, but—well—what did you call it when every blue BMW that went by, even in New York, made her quiver with the hope that Ken was at the wheel? *Esperar,* "to hope." If Chance kept on improving, she could truly hope to get out of Limit at Woolcott. *Probar,* "to try." She was still going to try to handle it all.

• • •

By now, Chance greeted Lucy's footsteps with his own peculiar soft whinny. The carrot she held out to him was a bit rubbery after a day in her knapsack, but he didn't seem to mind.

Frank had been right about learning from this horse. She'd focused on his training instead of her own performance and somehow both had improved. Chance was now working over three-foot fences, and he barely tried to turn his head at all. Obviously he'd been schooled well for years before the accident. How could anyone have given him up!

Riders getting ready for Woolcott crowded the ring. Even Eleanor was going to the show, entering Pipsqueak in Amateur Owner, though Lucy wondered why Frank had agreed. Lucy made a point of checking the ring entrances each time she passed, to guard against any sudden surprises for Chance. People weren't always careful how they cut into the line of moving horses.

"All right, Lucy," Frank called. "Let's give it a go."

The first round of jumps went perfectly. Even the "in and out"—two fences only a stride apart—caused no problems.

"Walk him a bit and we'll do it again," Frank said, starting to raise a rail.

A few minutes later Lucy cantered a slow circle and rode up the first line of fences. As she looked ahead to the second line, a big horse with a shrieking older woman hanging on his neck came rearing and plunging from the back entrance. Chance spooked and crashed into the next fence. "It's okay, fella. It's okay," Lucy said, trying to sound calm, but she was badly shaken. By the time she'd brought Chance under control, they were at the other end of the ring. After all her work and only four days before the show. And by now the rider who'd caused the trouble was trotting along merrily.

Meanwhile Frank had reset the jump. "Bring him back here and take this fence again. Don't waste any time," he urged.

But when Lucy approached the fence, Chance wasn't having any part of it. He planted his feet and refused.

"Use your stick on him."

Lucy froze. How could she punish the horse for

something that wasn't his fault? He was blind in one eye and scared. It would be cruel.

Frank hurried over. "Lucy, do you care about that animal or not?"

"Of course," she snapped.

"Then make a circle and bring him back to the jump. If he hesitates at all, use your stick and tell him you mean it. Discipline doesn't have to be harsh. Use it fairly, to explain what you expect."

There was nothing to do but follow Frank's orders. Lucy walked the horse away from the jump, talking to him steadily. She poured encouragement into her voice. "You can do it, baby. I'll help you." As they approached the jump again, she said a swift prayer that she wouldn't need the crop. But no such luck. Suddenly Mr. Kendrick's voice seemed to join with Frank's. "You've done so much with that horse. Don't lose it now." She lifted her stick and twice brought it down sharply behind her leg. Afraid of the fence, Chance jumped at least a foot too high, but he made it. Pulling back to a walk on the other side, Lucy wondered about her softhearted reaction. She wouldn't have hesitated to teach another horse. Chance's handicap, thanks to Frank, hadn't been allowed to keep him from learning.

"A good correction, Lucy. Now take him in."

Darlene rode up alongside on Orion. "Too bad about the collision, but you really handled it well. Want to go to the Deli after we put the horses away?"

"Sure, if we can get back in time for my train," Lucy said happily. Now that Melissa was madly in love with Timothy, her *Carousel* costar, she was almost never at the barn. It would be great to have someone to talk to, especially someone else who was serious about riding.

"Meet you in the office," Darlene said, walking off on Orion. "I've got to tell my mother I'm using her car."

Lucy hurried to take off Chance's saddle and bridle. She led him outside through the door at the end of the aisle. The Oak Ridge property ended just yards from the barn, and walking the horse dry, Lucy thought longingly of Up and Down Farm set in acres of green fields. She turned to face Chance.

"Baby, try to remember what you learned today," she pleaded. "We just can't have problems at Woolcott. I'll bet Mr. Kendrick will be there." Chance took several steps forward and buried his head under her arm. He'd never done that before. Maybe it was some sort of a promise.

• • •

As they drove along the country road to the Deli, Darlene looked straight ahead. "Have you seen your father lately?"

"No. Not in a few months. We were together two weeks at spring vacation, so I didn't miss him so much for a while. But I spoke to him a few days ago on my birthday, and now—"

"Remember how I told you I wasn't allowed to see my father?" Darlene was still looking straight ahead. Her face was expressionless, as usual. "Well, I had dinner with him last night. He's a great guy, Lucy, and I'd missed him so much. My mother just used me to get more money out of him, and I found out she even told him I didn't want to see him."

"So how did you get together finally?"

"Dad got a court order. I guess he's really bitter

about Mother, but he wants to help me. And I don't see why he shouldn't. He's my father."

Darlene looked into the rearview mirror. "What do you think, Lucy? Am I being disloyal to my mother, if he won't support her but he wants to help me?"

Again Darlene looked into the mirror.

"There's hardly any traffic, Darlene, why do you keep looking in back?" Lucy started to turn around, but Darlene reached over to stop her.

"There's a man behind us who keeps driving closer but doesn't pass. That's strange on an empty road. Besides, he's wearing a baseball cap and dark glasses."

Lucy could hear a car moving closer. "Do you recognize the car?"

"No." The strawberry patch on Darlene's cheek was turning red.

Lucy checked her seat belt. Darlene's was fastened too. Suddenly there was a thud against the rear bumper.

"Oh, no," Darlene gasped.

Lucy reached for the dashboard as a second thud brought the seat belt tight against her stomach.

"What'll I do?" Darlene squealed, but she steadied the wheel and stepped on the gas.

"You're doing fine! Try to get to that stretch with lots of houses. Maybe someone will pull out of a driveway."

But a maroon car moved up next to Darlene and pressed them toward the soft ditch along the side of the road. With a lurch the wheels under Lucy's side of the car slipped off the road and she fell against the door.

"He's taking off," Darlene said.

Lucy sat up fast. She'd get the license plate this time for sure. She said the numbers out loud several times.

"There's pencil and paper in the glove compartment," Darlene said. "Write it down."

Lucy tore off the piece of paper with the number and put it in the pocket of her jeans. "Did you recognize the make of the car?"

"I think it was a Buick. Put down maroon Buick."

"Obviously someone was trying to scare us. But how did he know we'd be coming along just then?"

Darlene was resting against the back of the seat. "I saw the car pull out of the parking space opposite the stable. You know, where the town tennis courts are. But it took me a while to realize he was actually following us."

"I still don't get it," Lucy said. "It was just a fluke that we happened to start out for the Deli."

"It had to be the car," Darlene said softly. "It's Mom's car."

"You mean someone was just sitting there waiting for her car to pull out on the way home?"

Darlene hung her head. "Don't tell my mother. Please, Lucy. Don't say anything at all. Leave it to me."

"Sure. I'll give you the license plate number. But *tell* her. Something worse could happen."

It would be easy, Lucy thought, to wait for a particular car to pull out of Oak Ridge at the end of the day. It had to be the car. When the man started after them, there was no way of knowing who was inside.

"Darlene, did your mother ever find out who slashed her tires?"

"No. She insisted it was my father, and maybe she was right. He's been really furious at her."

Lucy thought back to that evening when Jean had rushed outside to check the damage. Frank had been the one to mention Jean's ex-husband, and Jean seemed to seize on the suggestion with relief.

"It can't be your father behind this today. He knows you go home with your mother and he wouldn't try anything with you in the car. Someone may be trying to scare your mother, but I don't think it's your father."

Darlene looked at Lucy. Her eyes seemed very large. "Who, then?"

"I don't know." Lucy felt embarrassed after sounding so positive. "One thing's sure, though—you're a really good driver. You never lost control of the car for a second."

"I've been driving over a year. How about you?"

"I'll be getting my license this summer when we go back to Connecticut."

"So you got your wish," Darlene said.

Lucy looked at her in surprise. "You remembered."

"Things may get better for me too. My father wants to send me to college, and he says he'll pay for some of the riding. If he does, Mom will have it easier."

Lucy started to laugh. "Do you realize how silly this is? The two of us are sitting here in a ditch talking about our broken homes. Do you feel okay about getting us out of here?"

Darlene started the motor and the wheels gripped the dirt. As the car bucked onto the road, Lucy felt shivers race up the back of her neck. Could this warning possibly have been meant for her? Of course not, she thought quickly. Everyone knew that she usually left the stable in a cab. But someone was getting meaner than messages in a notebook. If it was the same person, what was coming next?

• • •

Keeping quiet about the car episode wasn't easy. Lucy wasn't sure that Darlene would tell her mother or, if so, that Jean would go to the police. On the other hand, she didn't want her own mother or Ken in a flap about what was going on at the stable. By Thursday the memory was less intense. Shock had turned into determination to solve the mystery and soon.

To relieve the crowding in the indoor ring and to prepare the horses for the outdoor show, Frank had moved a number of lessons outside. Lucy worked hard with Chance and Stacy, too, since the schooling show was the morning of Woolcott. Chance handled all the new sounds well, but Stacy was mischievous and distracted.

Friday, when Lucy arrived at the stable, she found Stacy on the hayloft ladder around the side of the barn. She'd been told twice the day before that she wasn't allowed to be there. Lucy wondered if she'd let affection for Stacy and her closeness to Ken undermine her authority. Or was Stacy trying to avoid her lesson? Was she nervous about the show the next day?

When Lucy brought Tom Tom to the outside ring, Stacy was propping a huge Snoopy dog against the ring rail.

"What have you got there?" Lucy said sternly.

"He's my Snoopy. My pillows go inside him on my bed." Her brown eyes were fixed on Lucy. "He's going to watch my lesson."

"What's he going to see? Are you going to pay attention or fool around, like yesterday?" Lucy dropped to Stacy's eye level. "Tell me the truth, Stacy, are you worried about the show? You wanted to go so badly. But it's perfectly all right to wait for the next one."

Stacy kept her eyes on the dog. "I'm not scared, Lucy. I'm excited! My daddy and mommy *both* will be there."

"You've never brought Snoopy before. Why today?"

"He's my friend. You'll see. He'll help me pay attention."

Whatever the reason, the lesson went much better than the day before. Still, Lucy couldn't overcome the feeling that something was wrong. Stacy had no interest in helping to put Tom Tom away, but wanted to wait for Roger outside.

"No, Stacy," Lucy said. "I don't want to be responsible for you out here with the cars coming and going."

At the sound of a heavy truck turning into the driveway, Stacy changed her mind. "There's Rick. Okay, I'll wait in the office."

Lucy put the pony away and came into the office as Rick sailed through the front door. At the bulletin board Darlene and Cynthia were studying the Woolcott show schedule.

Stacy ran to Rick. "Any new jokes?" Her Snoopy dog was sitting behind the desk in Lucy's chair, his nose buried in a book.

"I haven't time for jokes today," Rick said, taking the hard hat nearest the door and sitting it on the top of his head. "I have to go to the horse show. See how I trot. And I can canter too." He looked pretty silly prancing around the room and up to the desk to leave his invoice. "I get the blue ribbon, right? I get the blue ribbon."

"Not from me you don't," Jean muttered.

Rick ignored her and cantered off toward the door. He hung the hard hat on its peg and exited with a bow.

"I can't stand that creep," Jean snapped.

"He's just foolish," Darlene said, leaving for the ring.

Roger, the Peisters' driver, poked his head into the office. Stacy jumped off the desk, scooped up Snoopy, and ran to him.

"Guess what's happening at our house today?" Cynthia said, strolling over to Lucy. "We're putting in a fancy burglar alarm system."

Lucy tried to move the conversation farther away from Jean, but Cynthia didn't budge. "I've been meaning to tell you," she went on. "Dad didn't mention it until now, but he was convinced that someone tried to break into the house. You know, the time we were supposed to be in Bermuda. Now he says he heard noises one night downstairs. When he threw all the lights on, they stopped. Later he saw marks where someone tried to jimmy a back window."

Lucy was painfully aware of Jean listening closely. She took a slow breath and tried to sound casual. "I guess you were luckier than Melissa and Jill."

There was nothing else she could think of to say. If Jean was involved in the robberies, she'd heard too much already. Lucy struggled to keep her eyes from the hard hats by the door. Cynthia had just proven they were a message system after all!

The office door burst open. Ken rushed over to Lucy, his cheeks flushed and his hair falling over his face.

"Guess what. My father's Strad has been stolen! There are police and reporters all over the house."

"Ken, that's terrible! You mean the house was robbed?"

"That's awful," Cynthia joined in.

Even Jean looked concerned. "When did it happen?"

"No one's sure. Dad was in New York yesterday seeing his manager, so he didn't go into his study. In fact, no one was in the house most of the day. This morning there were meetings about a TV program, so it was four o'clock before he decided to practice. The Strad was gone. One of the finest old violins in the world. I can't believe it."

"Is anything else missing? Have you checked the house?"

"They're just getting around to that now."

Lucy followed Ken outside and they hugged each other quickly. "That's what I came for," he said with a smile. "Besides, I had to get out of the house a few minutes. It's crazy over there."

"I'll bet," Lucy murmured.

Ken kissed her good-bye and rushed off to the car as Lucy stared after him.

Chapter Twelve

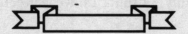

The sky was gray and the air quite chilly as they hurried from Ken's car to the Oak Ridge trailer on Saturday. The big open field, where the schooling show was taking place, was bleak in the early light. So this is what Ken looks like at six-thirty in the morning, Lucy thought. In his sleepy face she could see Ken Peister as a little boy.

"Stacy's lead line class opens the show and we need time to warm up," Lucy said, speeding up their pace.

Ken smiled over at his sister. "Her hair's cute that way, don't you think?" Two blond braids were tied with bright red ribbons.

"You look terrific, Stacy," Lucy said. "Your jacket is great with those jodhpurs, and my choker matches perfectly."

At the van Lucy collected Stacy's number from one of Frank's assistants. Stacy turned herself into a corkscrew trying to see how the white paper with the black number thirty looked on her back. Children with shiny faces rushed by on all sides. Distracted parents chased behind them.

Stacy pointed to a little girl nearby. "That kid gets to have a red ribbon on her pony's tail too!"

"That's a warning to tell you he kicks! Tom Tom's very well behaved."

Stacy studied her braids. After several seconds she said thoughtfully, "I think I'll wear green ribbons next time."

As they walked to the schooling area, Ken opened his camera and clicked away.

"I've promised Marina pictures before, during, and after," he said. "She was really disappointed about staying home. My father, of course, is glued to the phone."

"I heard a lot about the 'stolen Stradivarius' on TV. Do you think the reward will help?"

"Who knows? A famous Strad isn't easy to unload, and Dad said no questions would be asked. Nothing is missing but the violin, so this wasn't an ordinary robbery."

In the schooling ring Stacy was unusually silent, but she followed instructions well and Lucy was optimistic about the competition ahead. "Here goes," she said, with a wave to Ken, when the class was called. "We'll look for you at the rail."

Lucy led the pony into the ring at a snappy trot, then slowed to a walk at the announcer's instructions. Stacy's usual eagerness was missing, but after all, this was her very first class in her very first show. And she was surely disappointed that her parents weren't there.

When they won the blue ribbon, Stacy's smile reappeared. Waiting for them at the outgate, Ken looked just as happy.

Stacy reached for the ribbon. "Can I hold it?"

Ken unhooked the blue rosette from Tom Tom's bridle. "Of course. You earned it."

"It was easy. Lucy was with me."

Lucy removed the lead line from Tom Tom's bridle. "You'll do just fine, now, on your own. Let Ken hold the ribbon because your next class is coming up right away." The loudspeaker was already blaring, "Class three to the ingate, please. Beginners' Equitation, eight years and under. To the ingate, please."

Lucy led Stacy back to the ring. "Just remember three things. One: concentrate—think about what you're doing. Two: don't bunch up—stay away from the other ponies so you don't get kicked and the judge has a better chance to see you. Three: have fun. Ken and I will be standing at the rail right over there. You shouldn't talk to us, but I can whisper to you."

When Stacy walked Tom Tom into the ring, Lucy might as well have been in the saddle behind her. She was making every move and drawing every breath with the solemn little girl. Solemn. That was the trouble. Stacy was usually so full of spirit. Of course it was new to be riding on her own with eight other children, but . . .

Lucy joined Ken at the rail and they both smiled broadly as Stacy passed. Stacy managed a tiny half smile.

"She's not herself today, Ken."

"Go easy, Lucy. She's a little kid and she's never done this before. She's probably got too much to remember."

"It's more than that. You haven't watched her lessons. She's talented and fearless. She's riding well enough, but her sparkle's gone flat."

At the first canter Lucy groaned softly. Stacy was on the wrong lead. Half the class was wrong, but two of the kids corrected their mistake. Stacy didn't seem to notice until Lucy whispered to her from the rail.

"Line up, please," the announcer finally ordered. Several minutes later Stacy trotted out of the ring with a green ribbon for sixth place.

Lucy and Ken jogged to the outgate. "That was great, Stacy, really great for your first show," Lucy said as soon as they could get to her.

Stacy looked at Ken. "Can I go home now?"

"Sure. Is something the matter?"

"I just want to go home. I feel sick to my stomach."

Lucy helped her off the pony.

"I can get a lift with Frank," Lucy told Ken. "He'll be coming by later in the morning. Why don't you take Stacy home and meet me over at Woolcott at the Oak Ridge van."

She gave Stacy a hug. "You did very well and I'm proud of you. It was your first show and you're taking home two ribbons."

Stacy just looked up at Lucy with serious eyes. "Thanks for helping me." She started to pull off the choker.

"No, Stacy. I want you to keep it as a souvenir."

Lucy was glad to see at least a faint little smile as Stacy took Ken's hand and walked off.

● ● ●

When Ken showed up at Woolcott, Lucy had just climbed into the saddle for her second class.

"Say," Ken said, "this show is an altogether different operation from Stacy's."

"Sure. It's a B-rated show that runs for two days. Several classes go on at a time. There are temporary stalls, a refreshment stand . . ." Lucy pointed to the yards of green-and-white canvas that brightened the scene in spite of the weather.

"We're all having a great day. Come look!"

The Oak Ridge portable tack room was set up at the end of the van. Inside the gray-and-maroon-felt cubicle, Norman and Eleanor sat in two folding chairs, their coffee containers on a tack trunk between them.

"One of those red ribbons is mine—for Open on the Flat." Lucy pointed to a row of multicolored rosettes at the back of the booth. "It's hanging there for the glory of the stable but it goes home with me tonight. Second is the best I've ever done in an Open class."

Ken grinned at Lucy. "Open means anyone can ride no matter how many blue ribbons they've won. Flat means there are no fences to jump. How's that?"

"You get the blue for keeping things straight."

Darlene walked by on Orion. They looked like an equestrian magazine cover. "Has anyone got an extra bobby pin?"

"Right here," Jody said.

Jody was head groom for the show. Jean was working, too, rushing around, chin forward, keeping track of numbers and schedules.

"Can you come with me for a soda?" Ken asked Lucy.

"Sure. I'll ride over to the stand with you. Then I'll go to the schooling area from there."

"So Chance came through," Ken said as they walked along, dodging horses on the way to the ring.

"You bet! I've got so much to tell you. You know how worried I was about the noise around the ring with Chance's blind eye to the outside? Well, he was completely relaxed—weren't you, baby?" She leaned over and gave the gray horse a hug. "I kept a firm leg on him just in case, but he's done this all before. I'm sure of it. And his trust in me is awesome.

"Guess what else. Mr. Kendrick saw the class. He met me at the outgate for just a minute and then he had to run off, but we'll try to catch up later. Funny, Chance reminded him of a horse he'd seen before, but he couldn't remember where."

As Ken ordered a soda, Lucy heard someone call her name.

"Say, Lucy," Rick said as he approached the stand. "I see you're doing good. That's a nice gray horse you're riding."

"Rick! How come you're here?"

"I work some of the summer shows on the weekend. You know, deliver cases to the refreshment stands." He dropped two heavy cartons behind the counter and walked off to the truck a short distance away.

Ken offered Lucy a sip of his soda. "How's Melissa making out?"

"Not too well. She's been out of the ribbons all along."

"Is she disappointed?"

"I doubt it. She knows she hasn't been working."

Cole's such a fabulous horse, Lucy thought. He really deserves better.

"What are you thinking?" Ken asked.

"Forget it. Just sour grapes." Lucy listened to the loudspeaker. "I'd better get moving or I won't have time to school. My next class is the one I've got to win. I'll look for you at the rail, okay?"

Neither one of them moved. They just stood there looking at each other.

"I'd better get lost," Ken said abruptly, and they started off in opposite directions.

Now, *concentrate,* Lucy told herself as she trotted into the schooling ring. Frank was popping hard candies into his mouth like a fiend. He asked her to jump a few fences, then called her over. "You'll be fine, Lucy. Just think ahead. Anticipate your approach to each fence. No sharp turns. Give him plenty of time to see what's in front of him."

Lucy nodded. "I feel good, Frank."

She did too. Walking up and down beside the ring, Lucy watched about a dozen riders ahead of her. "Chance, if we stay cool and steady, we might take this class. I might just bring home *one* of those missing blues." She reached down and gave the horse a hug.

"Number sixty-two in the ring, please."

Circling slowly, Lucy felt Chance was as eager as she was to show what he could do. They moved around the fences at a controlled, even pace but with a sense of rhythm and style she'd never managed before. She tried to control her excitement as it built from fence to fence. When she rode the final circle at the end of the round, her heart was pounding. A better ride was a long way off.

"We did it, Chance," she said, stroking his neck. "It couldn't have gone better if you'd been Argus." Wasn't he the giant with a thousand eyes in the Greek myths?

Frank was at the outgate with Ken and Melissa behind him.

"Nice, Lucy," Frank said. "Never mind what the judge decides. You get the blue ribbon from me." He patted her boot. "I've got to get back. See you in the schooling ring before your next class."

The judge left the ring and Lucy felt suspended at the

top of a Ferris wheel. The loudspeaker crackled: "We have the winners of Class thirty-five. First, number sixty-two. Lucy Hill, Oak Ridge Stable."

She'd never forget this day, Lucy thought as she trotted into the ring. She reached for the ribbon before the ring steward could hook it on the bridle. "He's blind on that side," she said proudly. "I don't want him to spook."

When she left the ring, Ken was at the outgate beaming. "Congratulations!" He reached up and squeezed her hand. He patted Chance's neck. "What now?"

"I'm going to clean up Chance and leave him at the van. I'll look for Mr. Kendrick and get myself something to drink. Why don't we meet back here for Open? It's my last class for the day."

Lucy added her blue ribbon to the string in the tack room with a satisfied sigh. She was going well and the judge really liked her. Maybe—just maybe—she could take the Open class too.

At the refreshment stand she bought a soda and washed some of the ring dust out of her throat. Rick stood behind the counter holding two heavy cases on his shoulder.

"I'll take these back and bring more Diet," he said to the man behind the stand. Lucy walked with him to the truck.

"How's the day going?" Rick asked. "Too bad it's not sunny. We need thirsty people in our business."

"It's sunny enough for me. I won a blue ribbon!"

At the truck Rick steadied the cases on his shoulder while he opened the back of the truck. Then he shifted them onto the stacked cartons inside. Lucy froze. The weight on Rick's shoulder! The shifting motion to the truck! She'd seen it all before. She'd bet her blue ribbon that she'd just seen the match to that unforgettable image—the man in the hooded sweatshirt loading the TV set into the getaway van at Jill's.

Lucy stood motionless. Rick had been clowning with the hard hat in the office the other day. Was his act just an excuse to check the name tape?

"What's the matter, Lucy?" Rick said. "Have you seen a ghost?"

If only her face hid her feelings like Darlene's. All the time she'd been thinking, she'd just stared at Rick!

"I've got another class now," Lucy stammered. "See you."

Walk away naturally . . . calmly . . . she told herself. But she knew it wouldn't help. Rick had read her reaction. He must have seen her that night at Jill's. Now he knew she'd placed him at the robbery too.

Lucy's knees felt weak as she hurried to the van. Could she be rushing from one threat to another? Rick wasn't the only danger! How about his accomplice at the stable? Norman, Jody, Jean—her suspects were all here today.

"There you are, Lucinda!"

"Mr. Kendrick! Am I glad to see you!" In more ways than one, she thought.

"I missed your round but I heard that you won the class."

"Don't worry. You'll see me ride plenty before long. Mom says we'll be back in Connecticut sometime this summer."

Mr. Kendrick's face wrinkled with pleasure. "Frank's doing a fine job, but I won't be sorry to have you back. By the way, I think I've remembered about the horse you're riding. One of the girls from Michigan brought him to the National for the Maclay a few years ago. You've been lucky."

He put an arm over her shoulder. "We'll have plenty of time to catch up. I'll look forward to it."

As Mr. Kendrick hurried off, Lucy wanted to yell, Wait! Don't leave me! Her thoughts careened between fear and elation. Chance had been to the National!

Ellie came trotting by with a desperate look on her face. Jogging beside her, Norman shouted, "Lucy, can you help us here? Ellie's so nervous, she's forgotten how to steer."

Ellie's face was screwed up with tension. "What am I doing wrong?"

"Losing your cool, that's all." Lucy moved close to Pipsqueak's side. "Take a few deep breaths."

"Where's the schooling ring, anyway?"

"Over there. Come on, I'll show you." A few more minutes of protection!

Later Ellie begged to be taken to the ingate. "Otherwise I'll get trampled to death on the way."

The afternoon wasn't supposed to go like this, Lucy thought as she finally rushed back to the van. There was no time to school before Open Jumping, but at least she'd been safe.

Chance was tacked up and waiting. As Lucy hoisted herself into the saddle, Jody hurried to the van with another horse. "Sorry I wasn't here to help." She rubbed the dust off Lucy's boots.

"No problem."

When Lucy reached the ring, the first rider had already been announced. She was going fourth. As she stood near the ingate, Frank came running.

"Where were you?"

"I got into trouble," Lucy said, "and then it was too late to school."

"Well, forget it now. Do everything you did before. Go for it!"

Lucy rode into the ring with the same feeling of calm she'd experienced earlier. She knew Chance got most of the credit, a reliable partner beyond anything she'd hoped. Before she started her canter, she was pleased to see Ken at ringside next to Frank, Melissa, and some other kids from the stable.

But after the first fence, anxiety took over. The saddle felt loose. It couldn't be. She'd given the girth a hitch on the way to the ring. After the second fence she was sure something was wrong but she tightened her legs even more and moved on. Over the fourth fence the entire saddle swung sideways and Lucy went off on her head.

The cries at ringside stopped as suddenly as if a radio had been turned off. When the sound turned on again, Frank was kneeling beside her. The saddle was on the ground nearby.

"Are you all right?" Frank said. "Just lie there for a minute."

"I'm fine," Lucy said quickly.

Frank picked up the saddle and helped Lucy to her feet. Leading Chance, they walked out of the ring.

Ken and Melissa came running, but Lucy desperately wanted to be alone. She was furious and she needed to think.

"I'm really okay," she told them all. "Just let me go off by myself a minute."

Frank was examining the girth. "What the—!! Someone's cut the stitching between the elastic and the leather! Probably slipped a razor or a knife right between them. Lucy, did you leave the horse alone anytime after he was tacked up for the last class?"

"No," Lucy said.

No, but Jody did, she answered again, silently.

The show secretary came running. "Do you want the ambulance over here?"

"Nothing doing," Lucy said firmly.

The loudspeaker called Darlene's number to the ring. Frank handed the saddle to Ken. "I want to say a quick word to Darlene, but wait for me here. Lucy ought to be checked by a doctor."

Lucy took the saddle from Ken and insisted on going off alone. A short distance away she rested the saddle on Chance's back, reached under his belly for the girth, and tried to figure out what had happened. Of course Frank was right. The elastic end of the girth was still buckled in place. Between the elastic and the leather you could clearly see bits of cut threads. Probably just enough stitching had been left in place so that it would take a while for the girth to break loose. Had Rick done this while Jody was away from the van? Or had Rick told Jody about being recognized and left it to her?

Lucy began to feel confused. Her stomach was queasy. She felt Frank take her arm.

"Ken has gone for the car," Frank said. "He'll drive you to the emergency room at Woolcott Hospital."

At that moment Lucy was just glad there was someone telling her what to do.

Chapter Thirteen

"**F**eeling better?" Mrs. Hill said as she carried a dish of mandarin chocolate sherbet into Lucy's room the next afternoon. "I've brought you a treat. Your favorite!"

"That's great, Mom. Thanks!" Lucy reached for the dish and put it on the night table. "I really feel okay except for being totally bored. Why do I have to rest tomorrow too? I don't think I even had a concussion. I think the hard hat prevented it."

"You had a slight concussion and you know it," Mrs. Hill said. "The hard hat saved you from something worse!"

"Mom, let's call Dr. Petty and tell him I'm okay. Maybe he'll let me out tomorrow. I've got to get back to Oak Ridge."

"A few days away from the stable shouldn't be such a problem. School ends in a week and you'll be able to ride all you like." Mrs. Hill cocked her head toward Lucy's tape deck. "Isn't that the Haydn trumpet concerto?"

"Yes," Lucy said casually. "Ken gave me a batch of new tapes for my birthday. That's Wynton Marsalis playing the trumpet. Have you heard any of his jazz records?"

"Why—nooo. I'd like to."

Lucy hid a smile.

"Mom," she said carefully. "I haven't wanted to tell you but I got involved in another mystery and it's come to a head. When Ken brought me home from the show we agreed just to tell you I'd had a spill. I'd go into the rest later. Well, the truth is I fell because someone cut my girth and I think I know who did it."

Her mother was staring as though her eyes were glued open.

"There's something else," Lucy continued slowly. "A few weeks ago Darlene and I were run off the road by a car that was definitely trying to scare us. We got the license plate number so Darlene's mother could give it to the police, but I bet she didn't report it. I don't know how it's all connected yet, but I've got to find out."

Now Mrs. Hill was blinking rapidly. "You've got to go to the police up there, that's what you've got to do. Tuesday, Lucy. Not a day later. I'll go with you."

"Mom! They'll think it's ridiculous. A fifteen—I mean a sixteen-year-old girl telling them who's behind a chain of robberies—"

"Well, you can't go on with this by yourself, and that's final. You can practice telling your story to me if you like. I'd certainly be interested. But we're going to Oakdale on Tuesday. I'll arrange for an excuse from school."

Mrs. Hill leaned over the bed and kissed Lucy's forehead. "Missy, you mean too much to me to take any more chances."

"Hey, Mom! I haven't heard that nickname in years!"

As her mother left, Lucy flopped back against the pillow. She certainly didn't want to go to the police. Messages in a hard hat? They'd push her out the door for sure. If only she hadn't been so stupid about reacting in front of Rick. But at Jill's she hadn't reacted fast enough!

Rick had been the man in the hooded sweatshirt, she was positive of that. But who was supplying the names? Norman . . . Jody . . . Jean? Jean was certainly in the running. The two car episodes were baffling. "That louse! That louse!" Jean had wailed at the sight of the slashed tires. She'd definitely acted relieved when Frank suggested her ex-husband as the culprit. Maybe she'd been faking to throw people off the track. Who was the "louse" she'd thought of first? Could it have been Rick trying to scare her into some sort of cooperation? And was the shove into the ditch a more serious warning? No matter who'd been driving the Dodge—Jean or Darlene —the message would have been clear.

Lucy reached for the sherbet and, relishing the cool taste on her tongue, tried to recall times when Rick and Jean had been together. One afternoon Rick had been complaining about the "empties." She remembered thinking it was trivial. "Empties." Maybe Rick hadn't meant empty soda cans at all. Could he have been talking about empty houses? Could the tire slashing and the car scare have been his way of saying, "Keep coming up with more empty houses, or else"?

Any one of her suspects could easily have cut the stitching on the girth. All it took was a minute with a razor. Jody had had the most opportunity. On the other hand, Jody had been away from the van when Lucy picked up Chance the last time. Norman, Rick, or even Jean could have managed it then.

Lucky I wasn't using my new saddle, Lucy thought. That wouldn't have been any way to break it in!

Two minutes later Lucy went over the whole story again on the phone with Ken.

Two days later, far more cautiously, she told the same story to Lieutenant Ryerson of the Oakdale police.

• • •

Lucy was fascinated by the contrast between the quiet suburban station and the turmoil of the city precincts she'd seen shown in TV programs. She felt as though she were talking to the principal at school or someone in a bank.

To Lucy's surprise the detective listened to her patiently, making notes as she spoke.

"So let me get this straight. It was Cynthia Bernstein the first time and Jill Downes the second?"

"Yeah—I mean, yes. Then the next time there was no name tape at all."

"Can you remember if that was a Friday too?"

"I think so."

"And you're sure about the license plate on the maroon Buick?"

"Positive. I wrote it down a few seconds after I saw it."

"Well, thank you very much, Lucy. You're an observant young lady and you've been very helpful."

"Lieutenant Ryerson, do you think it's safe for Lucy to keep going to the stable?"

Lucy realized that this was the first time her mother had spoken during her whole recital. She hadn't even corrected any grammar.

"I wouldn't worry. We'll be watching out for her," Ryerson said matter-of-factly.

What could that possibly mean?

Mrs. Hill stood up and Lucy followed.

"I don't know what good that did," Lucy said when they were out on the street in Oakdale village. "But the detective was a pretty nice guy."

"It was the right thing to do, Lucy. Something *you* told him may fit together with what he already knows. But most of all, you'll be protected. I don't know what Lieutenant Ryerson plans to do, but I would guess he means what he says."

They crossed the street to the cabstand near the station. "You've done my bus and train laps," Lucy said to her mother. "Now for the end of the ride."

Since three other people shared the cab, there was little conversation, but after weeks of sitting next to strangers, Lucy liked having her mother beside her. At the stable it was fun to watch her mother meet the people who'd been so important in her life these past months. Mrs. Hill was friendly with everyone and really showed an interest in the horses. At Tom Tom's stall she remembered that this was the pony Stacy rode. She watched Darlene on Orion and admired Lucy on Second Chance.

Since Frank only let Lucy ride twenty minutes, it seemed as though they were back in a cab again minutes after they'd left one. But in another way they'd traveled to a different planet.

On the train Lucy looked over at her mother several times to find her lost in thought. Suddenly, Mrs. Hill squeezed Lucy's hand.

"I had no idea what a real strain this trip must have been three times a week. You're finishing up well at school. You managed to bring that half-blind horse along to where you were able to win a blue ribbon last Saturday. You've made new friends, including one interesting young man I'm eager to meet. And you're helping to solve the robberies at Oak Ridge. That's a lot to accomplish in about three months. Are you proud of yourself? I think you should be."

Lucy was startled. "Yeah, Mom. I guess I am proud of myself," Lucy said.

It was a minute before Lucy realized her mother had let the "yeah" pass.

"The word is yes," Lucy said in gentle imitation of her mother's usual tone.

"I thought better of it," Mrs. Hill said. "When I heard you correcting yourself in front of the lieutenant, I realized that you know the difference yourself. There's no point in my going on and on."

Lucy looked out the window to hide her reaction. But she turned back quickly and returned her mother's smile.

• • •

Later that night a phone call from Oakdale added to the day's surprises.

"It's Lieutenant Ryerson," Mrs. Hill called to Lucy. "He says he needs your help."

Lucy rushed to the phone.

"Yes, Lieutenant Ryerson?"

"Hello there, Lucy. There's something I'd like you to do for us. Have you paper and pencil handy?"

"Yes."

"Write down Phyllis Jaffe, Six Dolma Road. Got it? Now, can you imitate those block letters you described to me this afternoon and put the Jaffe name and address in the hard hat? Use the same ordinary masking tape. I want you to say no if you have any doubts about this."

Lucy was bursting with excitement. This was the first time in all her sleuthing she'd been asked to cooperate with the police.

"I can do it, Lieutenant. You mean next Friday, when Rick is due for his regular delivery?"

"Exactly. Wait until the afternoon if you can. We don't know what time of day they've been planting the tapes and we'd rather not be there ahead of them. If there's a tape in the hat already, memorize the address and call me from a phone outside the stable. Otherwise, put the Jaffe tape in place. And call me immediately if there's any trouble."

"It sounds as though you're going to stake out the Jaffe house."

"Good night, Lucy, and thanks. The less you know, the better."

Lucy hung up and started to call Ken. As usual, Mrs. Hill's typewriter was clacking in the background. She put down the phone and ran to tell her mother first.

Chapter Fourteen

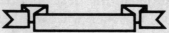

On Friday Lucy put the name tape in the hunt cap with no trouble at all. The days that followed were the problem. She wondered how the police were making out, and regardless of Lieutenant Ryerson's promise, she felt a little afraid.

School ended, and to Lucy's surprise she felt sentimental about Concord. Ken came into New York that day and finally met her mother. Later Lucy went out with him for a Japanese dinner and a movie. It was a perfect evening, but the last until his graduation.

The Stradivarius was still missing and the tension at the Peisters' grew worse each day. Stacy had been staying home from the stable, but Ken wasn't sure if she was suffering from a virus or the excitement in the house.

Between rides Lucy pushed the days along by puzzling about the identity of Rick's accomplice. Norman seemed to be hanging around more than ever. Jean was tense and irritable, but that was nothing new. Jody was completely confusing.

There was no question that Jody had slipped an envelope to Norman at the time of the videotaping. Then why had she pretended that she hardly knew Norman just fifteen minutes later? Jody had definitely acquired a used hi-fi set very recently. The biker she'd been arguing with looked tough enough to rob a bank, let alone an empty house. And what was the story about brother Patrick? Jody had certainly had the best opportunity to cut the girth at Woolcott. But then what was her connection to Rick? Were brother Patrick and the biker part of Rick's gang?

The trouble with all these notions was that Lucy wasn't convinced. She had an unshakable hunch that Jody could be trusted—that she was straight and kind and . . . maybe there were simple explanations for everything that looked bad.

Lucy thought of the night at the opera with Ken. Otello had come to a terribly unfair conclusion at just the sight of a white handkerchief. Was Jody, like Desdemona, the victim of the way things appeared? Had Lucy misinterpreted what she'd seen?

One morning, exactly twelve days after she'd planted the name tape, Lucy went to get Chance, hoping Jody would be working in his aisle. With school out there was more time to hang around, to try to find answers to some of her questions.

There was no one in sight, but something odd about Chance's whinny made Lucy uneasy. As she worked the bolt on his stall, she sensed someone moving behind her. Whoever it was must have come into the aisle from the door to the outside. Frightened, Lucy slipped into Chance's stall and put his big body between herself and danger. Then she looked back.

Jean stood at the stall door quietly, her eyes red from

crying. "I won't hurt you, Lucy. I'm in trouble, and I need to explain to somebody."

"Why pick me?"

"I think you've found out most of it already. Lucy, *please* come talk to me."

After all those days of silence in the office! "Why should I?" Lucy said. "You never had any patience with listening to *me*."

Jean's makeup was streaking and a comb was falling out of her hair. Her chin was almost to her chest.

"You were always around," she said. "I began to feel you could read my mind. I didn't know what I was getting into." Jean rushed on. "Rick just said about his brother-in-law selling security systems. I was supposed to get fifty dollars for each house that put in a system. If people were going away, they might need one. When the first house was robbed, I figured it was a coincidence. Even the second." Tears streamed down Jean's face. "I guess I didn't want to know. I needed the money. Then when I really got scared, Rick said I was already in trouble with the police and I couldn't quit or I'd be in trouble with him too. You know what happened. He slashed the car tires to show me. He got someone to chase you and Darlene."

Lucy's curiosity won out. She walked to the front of the stall. "How did you give him the names?"

"I think you figured it out."

Lucy clenched her teeth, determined to make Jean tell her more.

"In the beginning I just read him the names from my cards. But when I discovered what I was into, I didn't want anything to do with that rat. I just put the tapes in the hat. I didn't even have to talk to him."

"How about the payoff? How did you get the money?"

"Rick mailed it. I couldn't call him at home, or his wife would have raised the devil."

"So what do you want me to do?"

Jean sniveled. "You're a decent kid, Lucy, and a friend of Darlene's. You wouldn't want her mother to go to jail. Just make sure people know what really happened. Tell them it was Rick's fault."

Footsteps sounded against the concrete. They were heavier than Jody's. Lucy shifted her position so she could see into the aisle. Norman was walking toward them with long, deliberate strides. He was a powerful man who could knock anyone out with one chop to the neck. Lucy's stomach tightened and shivers ran up her back. Had she let herself get trapped between two criminals who meant more harm than a spill from a horse?

"Okay, Jean. Let's wrap this up." Norman looked at Lucy, then back to Jean. Lucy was about to scream, but the sound stuck in her throat. Then Norman grabbed Jean's arm and flashed a police badge. Lucy fell back against Chance in surprise.

"We've got Rick," Norman said. "You'll have to tell your story at headquarters." Lucy sagged against the horse with relief as Jean burst into tears.

"Lucy," Jean whimpered, "tell them I didn't mean it. Tell them."

"You can talk for yourself," Norman said, marching Jean along the aisle.

Suddenly Chance put his muzzle over Lucy's shoulder. She reached up for his nose. "I suppose you want to know what's going on," she said. "Well, I don't understand much more than you do. And what I know, I'm too knocked out to tell you."

• • •

Rumors raced through the stables the rest of the day. Everyone noticed that Jean wasn't there and a number of people had seen her taken away. Lucy knew better than to talk about the case. She'd been cautioned about that last summer when charges were pending in the mystery at Up and Down Farm. But she hoped Norman would get back to the stable before the end of the day. She was bursting with questions.

At five-thirty Frank stopped her in the tack room. "Meet me in the office, Lucy. I'll be there in a minute, and Norman wants to see you."

How much did Frank know about this? Did he realize that Norman was a cop?

Frank smiled at her. "Go along, Lucy. You'll get all the answers to your questions very soon."

Lucy walked across the stable entryway and opened the door to the office. Ken and Melissa were standing by the extra desk. It was covered with a paper tablecloth and a spread of foods from the Deli.

"Surprise!" they shouted.

"You're a heroine," Melissa said.

"What is this?" Lucy said, turning red. "Sa-ay! Brownies! Cheese! Even artichoke hearts! You two really know me."

"Frank arranged it," Ken said. "He left us pretty much in the dark, but I gather you solved the mystery."

"Not really..I was off base most of the time. Can you believe it, Norman's—"

"Take the credit, Lucy," Frank said as he walked into the office. "Norman says you earned it."

"Did you know about Norman from the beginning?" Lucy asked. "And is he really Eleanor's boyfriend?"

"Yes to the first. No to the second." Frank helped himself to a brownie and took a big bite. "After so many of the Oak Ridge families were robbed, I began to think it was more than a coincidence. When I talked to the police, they thought it was worth a look. Ellie's been around here for years. She agreed to act as Norman's cover."

"She was a pretty good actress, if you ask me," Melissa said. "It must have been a terrific nuisance at times."

"Go on. She loved it. Ellie's full of fun and it was all a great big laugh."

"Where's Darlene? I haven't seen her around."

"She went to see her father to try to raise Jean's bail. That's one good kid. I'm glad she's got horses in her life."

Lucy knew what he meant. Darlene had faced a lot of pain, but it could all be left behind when she climbed on a horse. Lucy had learned that firsthand. But Darlene's situation made her almost ashamed at how sorry she'd felt for herself at times. Her own family situation was actually pretty terrific. Even if her parents were apart, they pulled together for her. And they were neat people —*both* of them.

Lucy popped open a can of soda. "Jean was really pitiful when she talked to me this morning. She said she was misled by Rick in the beginning and then she was stuck. She was like someone on a lead line, going where Rick pulled."

"You've got a kind heart, Lucy," Ken said with a fond smile. "But look at all the trouble she's caused."

"She shouldn't have climbed up on the horse in the first place," Melissa said. "Do you think Jean will go to jail, Frank?"

"Ask Norman. That's probably his car in the driveway."

"What do you think?"

"I think it depends on whether or not anyone believes her story."

Sometimes it's hard to know what to believe, Lucy said to herself, thinking of Jody.

Norman sauntered through the door. "Well, Frank, I guess we wrapped it up. I can get out of the way." His manner wasn't all that different as a detective than it had been as Ellie's boyfriend. He turned to Lucy. "And this kid was a big help. Sa-ay, Melissa. Jody has something for you in her car. She left the police station right behind me."

"Give me a break," Lucy exclaimed. "Don't tell me Jody's a cop—a policewoman too!"

Frank and Norman broke up. "She's going to be a dental technician," Frank said, "but her mother needs her at home right now so she's taken a year off from school. We let her in on our problem about three months ago when we found out Jean's lists to me were incomplete—"

"What lists?" Lucy asked.

"Each week Jean made a list for me and the grooms of the people who were going to be away."

Those lists, Lucy thought. She supposed it wouldn't be tactful to tell Norman he'd dropped one by the pay phone.

"Rick must have known we were on his tail," Frank went on. "He probably told Jean not to include the name that was in the hard hat, just in case the police were watching all those houses."

"So how did Jody come into it?"

Norman took over. "The boarders always let Jody know when they were going to be away. They're all crazy about her. A few weeks ago Mrs. Cooper even gave her the hi-fi set they were replacing in the living room."

So the explanation was just that simple.

"Frank, have you known Jody long?" Lucy said.

"About ten years, I guess."

"And her older brother, Patrick? Did he ride here too?"

"For a while. Then he got interested in playing ball." Frank's face turned grim. "He won't be playing anything much anymore."

"Wasn't he the guy in that terrible wreck about a year ago?" Ken asked. "The White Plains paper was full of it."

"Yeah! Patrick was in a car with a real rotten apple. His friend, if you want to call him that, was drunk and stoned. He just walked away, but Patrick's a paraplegic for life. Jody adored her brother and couldn't believe he'd been running around with this guy. The family won't give Patrick his letters, so the guy comes over here a few weeks ago on his monster motorcycle to get Jody to deliver something for him."

"Maybe he's sorry."

"Don't count on it, Lucy. He's just no good. He's not allowed to ride that motorcycle with his license revoked, but I couldn't do anything about it without blowing my

cover. You can bet I'll catch up with him now! He's—"
Norman stopped himself as Jody came through the door.

"Say, Jody. Remember the package you were going
to drop off at the Townsends'? Is it still in your car?"

Jody nodded and left again quickly.

"Norman, I've still another question," Lucy said.
"Why didn't *you* plant the Jaffes' name and address in
the hard hat? Why did Lieutenant Ryerson ask me to
help?"

"That one's easy. I'd been hanging around the office
too much already. You had an excuse to be there anytime."

Jody came back into the office and held a brown
paper bag out to Melissa. "Your name is on it. We decided to bring it back to you ourselves."

Melissa opened the bag and drew out a large silver
box.

"Don't tell me you found the loot!" Lucy exclaimed.
The box was tarnished, but Melissa's shining face made
up for it.

"Listen to her." Norman laughed. "She sounds like
bad television. Yes, Lucy, Rick led us to a good part of
the loot, trying to cut himself a break—"

"Dad's violin—" Ken broke in. "Was it there? Did
you find it?"

"Most of the expensive stuff was collected in one
place. Maybe they were going to wait to unload it until
more time had passed. Or maybe they didn't know how
to unload it. These guys weren't big-time crooks. . . ."

Ken's face told Lucy that he already knew what Norman was going to say.

"But no, Ken. Your father's violin wasn't there."

Chapter Fifteen

After three months of racing for trains, it was a pleasure to stroll through Grand Central the next morning with time to spare. Lucy stopped to browse at the newsstands and gawk at the beautiful ceiling. She treated herself to a frozen yogurt and settled down on the train to the luxury of reading a mystery just for fun. But her mind kept wandering to Ken and to Stacy. If only Mr. Peister could find his violin and let the family get back to normal. Lucy was really worried about Stacy. Last night's bulletin from Ken was impossible to believe.

"You mean she's really not coming to the stable ever again?" Lucy had protested.

"That's what she says."

"She couldn't have lost her nerve. Not Stacy."

"She's not acting like Stacy," Ken had complained. "She's quiet and she still says she's sick to her stomach. Besides, she's practicing the violin for hours without being told. Of course, Dad is thrilled but . . . it's not Stacy."

Lucy thought back to the first time she'd met the little girl. She'd known right away that she was a natural rider.

She'd been brash and perky. What had happened to the sparkle and the spunkiness? The wrong lead at the show had been a big surprise. Stacy and Tom Tom almost always got that right. Certainly Stacy should have noticed that the lead was wrong. If nerves had been her problem, why hadn't she been fine when her classes were over? Instead she'd wanted to go right home. Had the disappointment about her parents just killed all the fun?

Come to think of it, the change in Stacy really started just before the horse show. She'd played on the hayloft ladder when she knew she shouldn't. She'd brought her Snoopy to the stable and . . . Lucy sat up straight. Wait a minute—was that a clue?

The rest of the train ride seemed as long as the flight to California. At the Oakdale cabstand Lucy begged the starter to put her into a cab alone, but too many people were waiting. She just about pushed the taxi all the way to the Oak Ridge driveway.

Seconds after the cab stopped, Lucy was at the hayloft ladder. Halfway up, she heard Frank yell from the ring. "Lucy Hill, what the devil are you doing up there?"

"Trust me, Frank, *please.*" She climbed higher.

Lucy stepped into the dark hayloft and tried to imagine what Stacy would have felt. If the dim light had made her timid, she would have chosen a spot near the front. But she was a smart kid. She'd probably have realized that the front bales were used first. She'd have scrambled up the low bales that were stacked like steps to a high spot in back. No, her legs were probably too short.

One side of the loft was empty. Lucy felt her way along a row of bales until she reached the back wall. There was a bit of space between the wall and the last stacks of hay. Could Stacy have crawled in there? The only way for Lucy to find out was to lie on her stomach and reach as far as she could. She stretched out her hand behind the bales and struck something hard.

For several moments Lucy just lay on the wooden floor, weak with relief. Then she worked the case toward her until she was able to grab the handle. For a crazy moment she thought she'd made a mistake. All the violin cases she'd ever seen were shaped like violins. This was a long rectangle, covered in some kind of black leather. Then she picked up the case and made her way to the front of the loft. She started down the ladder.

● ● ●

"Ken? Ken! I'm so glad you're home," Lucy said from the pay phone by the soda machine. "Can you come to Oak Ridge right away? Drop what you're doing and get here fast. It's important."

"For Pete's sake, what's up? Are you all right?"

"I'm fine. But, Ken, *please.* Get into your car and get over here."

"Sure. Sure."

She was about to hang up. "Wait! Ken? I'll meet you down at the road."

"Lucy? What on earth is—"

She hung up before he could go on.

With a positive stride, as though carrying nothing but a school briefcase, Lucy walked down the stable driveway. The last thing she needed right now was to answer questions. Her hands and feet suddenly felt cold. She'd carried this priceless instrument down the hayloft ladder backwards holding on to the rungs with one hand!

She took a deep breath. The next step seemed almost

as risky. How was she going to make Ken understand what had happened? Even worse, Mr. and Mrs. Peister?

Lucy watched the road from the end of the driveway and again tried to think like Stacy. Once Stacy'd realized the trouble she'd caused, she must have been miserable, and—in that house—even terrified. Each day that passed, it must have been harder to tell the truth, and the longer she'd waited, the bigger her "crime." Lucy wanted to put her arms around Stacy right that second.

The BMW pulled up and Ken slammed on the brakes. "Wha—what have you got there?" he sputtered. He reached over to open the door for Lucy, then jumped out of the car instead.

"Wait," Ken said. "I'd better help you." Taking the violin, he ordered, "Fold the front seat down while I hold the fiddle. Good."

Carefully, Ken laid the case flat on the backseat. "Where, Lucy? How did you . . . We'd better get to the house right away."

"It's back, Ken. Aren't you excited about that?" Lucy was startled to see Ken so upset. She climbed into the front seat and put a hand to her forehead. "Please, could we go somewhere and talk first? Please!"

Ken looked at her warily but pulled into the public parking area across the road from the stable. He brought the car to a stop and looked at Lucy impatiently. "Now tell me where you found it."

"First let me explain what probably happened. You know how crazy Stacy is about her father—"

"Stacy?!"

Lucy rushed on. "She's wanted him to come to see her ride from the very beginning. She was determined to have him come to the horse show. Okay, she knows your father goes on concert tours. She's told me . . ."

Ken nodded as though in a trance.

"Well, she must have thought that if she hid his Stradivarius, he wouldn't be able to go. Today it came back to me that a few days before the show I caught her playing on the ladder to the hayloft a couple of times. She must have been checking out the loft. The day before the show your father was in New York, remember? Stacy came for her lesson with the chauffeur. Then she was at the ladder again. Later she brought a big floppy Snoopy dog down to the ring."

"The one from her bed?"

"Yes. I think she put the violin case between the pillows inside the dog and brought it to the stable. Classes were just beginning to move outside. She probably waited for Roger to pull out of the driveway and took the case up to the hayloft. By the time I saw Snoopy, the pillows were still stuffing him up but she must have stowed the violin."

"I don't believe this." Ken pushed the hair off his forehead and flipped it back again without noticing. "Do you realize the commotion she's caused? No wonder she's sick!"

"Will your parents freak out? I don't think she had any idea that it was such a big thing. She can't realize how valuable the violin is. She wouldn't understand even if you told her in dollars."

"I suppose not," Ken said more calmly. "But she knows how important it is to my father."

"I guess your father's just as important to her," Lucy said quietly.

Ken was silent for several moments. "Well, what do we do now?" he said finally.

"When does Stacy go to bed?"

"Eight o'clock."

"And will your parents be home tonight?"

"As far as I know."

"Well, suppose you phone them and say you're taking me to supper and that you'll be bringing me home with you around eight-thirty. Can we go down to the Deli until then?"

"Dad's Strad in the Deli?" Ken sounded genuinely shocked.

"Can you think of somewhere else to go? We'll watch it every minute."

Again Ken was silent. "Okay," he said. "I'm too spaced out to think." He smiled at Lucy for the first time and started the car motor. "You know what's really too bad? Dad had always planned to be home for the show. Stacy didn't have to go through this at all."

• • •

At the Deli Ken carried the violin to a booth and laid it on one bench while Lucy slid into the other. Moments later Darlene walked over.

"How are things?" Lucy asked her hesitantly. "I've been thinking about you."

"Yeah, well, it's okay, Lucy. Mom's had a hard time and she didn't use her head. But it will probably be all right. That's what my dad says. He got her a lawyer."

"I'm really glad, Darlene. I'll be around the stable for at least another month. Could we go out on the trails together?"

"Yeah—soon! Orion and I could use some fun!"

As Darlene walked away, Lucy looked at her watch. It was only six-thirty. The next hour and a half was really strange. How could the minutes drag for two people who never had enough time together? Somehow the black case on the opposite bench seemed to rob them of words. At last Ken announced that it was time to go and they reached the Peisters' at eight thirty-five. Ken locked the violin in the car and closed the heavy garage door behind it.

Mr. and Mrs. Peister were in the living room when Lucy walked in behind Ken.

"Good evening, Lucy," Marina said. "Ken—is something the matter?"

"Could we sit down and talk?"

"Of course." Marina pointed to the couch that faced her. She began to turn a ring around and around on her finger.

Mr. Peister's face was stern. Lucy tried to send Ken mental waves of moral support.

"Uh—Dad," he started. "We want to explain a few things about Stacy. She's done . . ." He stopped as Mr. and Mrs. Peister looked at each other with alarm.

"She's done something outrageous," he went on, "but there was no way she could understand the consequences. She just thought she'd found a neat way to make sure her father was home for the horse show." The last words fell over each other in a rush.

Mr. Peister looked at Marina in disbelief. Then he fixed Ken with an icy stare. "Are you telling me that your sister stole my violin?"

Before Ken could answer, Mr. Peister stood up abruptly. He seemed to be actually shaking, though Lucy wasn't sure if it was relief or fury.

"Where's the fiddle?" he demanded. "Ken, where is it?"

"Locked in the BMW in the garage."

"Have you lost your mind!"

"Ken, I'm surprised," Marina chimed in. "After two and a half weeks of incredible strain—"

"Don't stand there. Get it!" Mr. Peister exploded, and Ken hurried from the room.

Embarrassed, Lucy couldn't decide whether to keep absolutely still or to try to help in some way. She wished she weren't there, but she wouldn't have wanted Ken to face this alone.

Marina spoke first. "Did you find the violin, Lucy? Or did Stacy tell Ken about it?"

Lucy started to answer when Ken came back. Mr. Peister snatched the case and laid it on the couch. The room was deadly silent as he lifted the top. Cradled in pale blue silk was the most beautiful violin Lucy had ever seen. The light-colored wood actually glowed. Mr. Peister lifted the instrument from the case and examined it lovingly front and back. He scrutinized the black pegs and strummed the strings once or twice. It was as if the violin was actually a part of himself.

How could an eight-year-old possibly understand? Lucy swallowed hard, wondering what was going to happen next.

Mr. Peister turned to Ken. He looked gray and exhausted. "She'll have to be punished, Ken. It's a serious thing."

"I know, Dad. I just wanted to explain that it didn't seem that way to Stacy."

Mr. Peister went on as though he hadn't heard. "And

Miss Hill here. Lucy. I assume you found the violin where Stacy hid it?"

"That's right, Mr. Peister. In the hayloft at the stable."

Mr. Peister turned to his wife quickly. "How on earth did it get there?"

"In the big floppy dog from her bed. The one she keeps her pillows in," Lucy answered.

A faint smile formed at the corners of Mr. Peister's mouth. "No wonder she's been sick for two weeks. With all the press around the house, the bulletins on TV . . ." His voice trailed off.

Lucy got up her courage. "Mr. Peister, has Stacy ever been to one of your concerts?"

"No, Lucy," Marina said quickly. "Fritz doesn't believe in taking children until they can sit still without disturbing other people."

Ken jumped in. "That's just it, Dad," he said. "There's no way she could understand. The famous people Stacy's friends talk about are TV stars or tennis players. She hears you play the violin around the house. It's just what you do."

Mr. Peister's long face was beginning to relax. He returned the violin to the case and carried it out of the living room. Again Lucy sat in silence. In the next room Mr. Peister was talking to someone named Bronislaw, who seemed to be his manager. Yes, the violin was back. No, there would be no further information. They'd talk in the morning about what to tell the press.

"Marina, I'll talk to Stacy," Mr. Peister said when he came back into the room. "She'll have to be punished. Let's say she can't ride for two weeks or perhaps you'll think of something else. But I want you to call Bronislaw back tomorrow morning and arrange to have Lucy, Ken, and Stacy in our box at Carnegie Hall on the twenty-eighth. I hope you will be able to join us that night, Lucy." He turned to leave the room. "I'm going upstairs to see if Stacy's still awake."

• • •

"Carnegie Hall is so elegant and . . . well . . . friendly, compared to the Met," Lucy said to Ken as they sat in the center box behind Mrs. Peister and Stacy. She liked the simple cream-colored background decorated with just enough gold, the sweeping circles of seats above the orchestra, bordered with red velvet and rimmed with light.

Applause rippled through the hall and Mr. Peister walked out onto the stage. Stacy was astonished. "Are they clapping for Daddy?" she whispered. Lucy and Ken exchanged a look as the audience clapped on and on. Finally Mr. Peister gently raised a hand. The audience gradually settled down, and he put his violin under his chin.

As the beautiful sound poured out of the precious Stradivarius, Lucy was grateful for her part in bringing it back. She was spellbound by the hush in the hall, the shared enjoyment that seemed to link hundreds of strangers, and the wonderful interweaving of the violin and piano in one melody after another.

The emotion of the music nudged Lucy's feelings in all sorts of directions. What an amazing few months had just gone by. In one week Ken would be leaving for England to see his mother. Lucy was going to miss him terribly and hoped he could somehow cut his visit short.

At least she and Chance were starting in the Maclay group at Oak Ridge next Monday and that would help.

Lucy had to admit that the move back to Connecticut was going to be a little sad. She would really miss Allison —and New York too. The energy and variety of the city were no longer frightening.

The sonata ended, bringing Lucy back to the hall. As the extravagant applause was joined by cries of "Bravo!" Stacy looked at her brother as if to say "Did you know about this?" She sat surprisingly still through the rest of the program and was especially excited by one of the short encores, "The Flight of the Bumblebee."

"Daddy's playing that piece for you," Marina whispered.

"Of course," Stacy answered. "He always does."

As the applause went on and on, Mr. Peister came back for one bow after another. Finally the houselights brightened and the concert was over.

Mrs. Peister led them backstage past a line of people that stretched the length of the building. "What are they waiting for?" Stacy asked.

"They're waiting to see your father."

"But why? Do they know him?"

"In a certain way," Marina said. "They want to thank him for the concert and to shake his hand or ask him to autograph their programs."

Stacy looked up at Marina. "I want him to autograph *mine.*"

Before long Mr. Peister was surrounded by his admirers in a room backstage. Ken explained that meeting the performer in the so-called "green room" was an old custom in the theater. Looking around the buzzing crowd, Lucy realized that the music world, with its own superstars and special traditions, meant as much to a lot of people as the riding world meant to her.

"Thank you," she said, pressing Ken's hand. "I've really enjoyed tonight."

Her mother had always been right in a way, Lucy thought. Nothing could ever be as important as riding, but there were so many other things to know about. She'd be more adventuresome in the future. But, remembering Jean and Rick at Oak Ridge, she'd make sure to watch out for false leads.